I am sensitive and i

I wonder why we are here

I hear music from the soul

I see a beautiful future, only it's too far away

I want the world to fix itself

I am sensitive and imperfect...

I pretend that my veins don't burn with rage at all the injustices in the world

I feel voices of a better future breezing past my ear in sweet song

I touch the light within me and reach out to find it in others

I worry that things will be the same for generations to come

I cry when the beauty of hope shines through the dark curtain of despair

I am sensitive and imperfect...

I understand that in the end love will save us all

I say anything is possible because everyone can change

I dream of the world actualising the ideal

I try harder than everyone else

I hope that one day it will all make sense

I am sensitive and imperfect...

...I am Jack

1

Now

They say that when you die your entire life will flash before your eyes. This was only half true for Jack.

His life did indeed flash before his eyes, but it was not the life he lived which he witnessed in his final moments.

What passed before his eyes was the future that he often dreamt of. All he wanted to one day live up to, all those aspirations, now gone, never to be reached.

"I love you" he hears his mother whisper to him from the side of his hospital bed.

His life had been a miserable waste. He didn't have the best relationship with his parents, they were strangers to him on a good day, but it was comforting to have them here now.

Next to her, his dad also whispers "I love you son".

These are to be the last words that he would ever hear.

Sound soon becomes more and more distant once these words are spoken, as though everything audible is hauled away by a silent train heading for distant shores.

Jack feels as though he is inside an elevator, no longer able to keep his eyes open, and there is nothing he can do to stop it. He is its passenger and his consciousness is descending along with it.

'Goodbye... I'm so sorry to be leaving you... You were my family, but I wasn't meant for this world... This world was all wrong...but I don't want to leave...'

Jack wakes up.

He opens his eyes to find himself lying by a stream in the most beautiful forest that he has ever seen.

It is a gorgeous sunny day, blessed by the lovely golden rays of light which beam down to brighten everything with the warmth that makes life worth living.

'What's this?' he asks himself, having no clue of where he is, or any memory of how he had gotten there.

The last thing he remembers was saying goodbye to his parents, just before going to sleep for that final time on the hospital bed.

His questions soon disappear however, when he lets them take a backseat to the views of the blooming grass and leaves around him.

The forest is alive with its many caterpillars, butterflies and bees, all breezing through the fragrant foliage. The sight of it all brings a tear to his eye having lived so much of his life indoors.

'Green! It's been too long since I last saw this precious colour of life!'

The tear marks his gratitude for having finally found a place which is not made from cement alone, and all that can be heard within the untouched silence, is the calming sound of the clear running water which trickles through the nearby stream.

Taking a deep breath to relax, in the hope of escaping his disorientation, Jack realises that the air here is different too. What he breathed in before had never tasted this good, it is so clean now, like sweet nectar bringing delight with every breath. Maybe he was imagining it, but he could feel himself getting better with each inhalation.

"Hi there!" a high-pitched voice unexpectedly calls over.

Jack looks round but sees no one. The sun shines so brightly however, that besides the stream and the plant life nearby, everything in sight is absorbed into a radiant glare.

Sunlight. It had been too long since he last felt its heavenly grace wash over his skin.

"I said hi there!" the voice calls over again, its pitch almost comical.

Jack again looks round, still seeing no-one through the light.

"Oh... Hi" he replies, not wanting to offend whoever is possibly addressing him.

"That's better" declares the voice in a dignified tone, "You know there's some clothes at the tree nearest you."

'Clothes?'

This takes his attention away from the forest for a moment, making him look down to suddenly realise that he is lying there on the grass with absolutely no clothes on.

The question *"How did I get here*?" comes to mind, but first thing first; Jack runs behind the tree and quickly gets himself dressed.

He soon steps out from behind the tree, and examines his new garments of a powder blue tee-shirt and trousers, with brown sandals.

'Not a bad fit' he thinks while studying them. He then pauses to reflect on what has just happened.

'I haven't been able to run, or dress myself, in a long time… My pain is gone too. How is this possible?'

He also begins to wonder how such good clothes that fit him so well had managed to get there in the first place.

His pondering is soon interrupted however, when a small ginger cat jumps out from nowhere to land at his feet.

The feline looks up at him with big vigorous eyes filled with the playful colour of mischief, eyes that tell a story of a beautiful scamp who knows her own intelligence. Then in the same high pitched voice from only moments ago, Jack hears the little cat say "Hello".

A bemused smile appears on his face.

'A talking cat! Now I've seen it all!'

"Don't you know it's rude to stare!" remarks the cat, her comical voice undoing the intimidating tone she is going for.

Not knowing what else to say to a cat, Jack asks her name.

"My name is Jasper" she replies, before turning away to clean herself.

Keeping with his unfaltering etiquette, which he did not reserve for humans alone, Jack decides to keep rapport going with his newfound friend. Maybe she could tell him where he was.

"Nice to meet you Jasper, my name is Jack".

Jasper continues to clean herself, but he believes there may have been a brief noise of acknowledgement.

He decides to follow up with another question.

"Can you tell me where I am?"

All expectations of finding out where he is hinge on Jasper's response, but like a typical cat she chooses to look the other way as she continues to clean herself.

'You may be talking, but you're definitely a cat!' he notes to himself, smiling at her classic feline behaviour.

Assuming that he has been dismissed, Jack walks out from under the canopy and back into the open grass for the sunlight to wash over him again.

The clear light invigorates his being, with a warm vitality that rinses away any stale energy which may have lingered.

With his eyes now adjusted a bit more to the brightness, Jack spots some fruit growing from a nearby bush and decides to go over for a closer inspection.

The strange fruit is red in colour and unlike anything he has ever seen before. Though now that he thought about it; he had never actually seen food growing before with his own eyes.

Eventually he decides to pick one for a taste.

"Hope this doesn't belong to anyone" he declares, before biting in through the fruit's crisp skin and down into its soft juicy centre.

"It belongs to you, fool" Jasper calls over, as he savours his first bite.

The fruit is delicious.

He finishes it quickly and the exotic mouth-watering taste remains, so strange and exciting.

Then with his eyes adjusted and his pallet satisfied, Jack looks up to find something very odd.

He had thought nothing of it at first because his eyes had been adjusting to the bright daylight which he was unaccustomed to, but now there is no denying what he could see.

Clear as day, where it should be blue, the sky above him is now orange.

He just stands there mystified, looking up.

"First there is a talking cat, now there's an orange sky! What's going on here?" he yells out.

As if in reply to his outburst, Jasper returns from under the canopy.

"I'm supposed to congratulate you".

"Congratulate?" he asks, confused at what he is to be congratulated for.

"Yeah, congratulations Jack! You have emerged from the fountain, and anyone who emerges from the fountain is to be congratulated".

"The fountain?"

"Yeah, the fountain. You are here for a reason, but your people can tell you more, I can take you to them if you like?" she offers.

"Sure...why not..." agrees Jack, not knowing what else to do.

8

With no memory of how he has wound up here, and no knowledge of where to go, an explanation would be nice. Having enlisted the cat's help was also reassuring.

"Follow me!" commands Jasper, turning away to abruptly strut off at pace, leaving Jack to hurry after this proud leader of the pack.

'What's wrong with this picture?' Jack reflects to himself, laughing at the situation.

'I'm walking under an orange sky, following a talking cat, through a weird forest, wearing clothes that aren't even mine!'

A bizarre situation indeed, but at least he is not alone. He believes there is a friendship growing between himself and his furry guide, he feels like he can trust her. Many people would never have followed a strange cat, or indeed believed the cat was actually talking to them in the first place, but Jack always kept one rule for times like these, and that was to follow your instincts.

Though he does begin to question whether the cat really is the cute little helper that he hopes her to be, as he struggles to keep up with her agility.

"When do you think we'll get there?" he calls over.

"When is now?" replies the cat in a lofty tone.

He continued to grow fonder and fonder of her by the minute. Nothing but witticisms had been exchanged between the two along their journey, insult-free witticisms of course. Most people would still have been annoyed even when the jibes were not insulting, however, Jack finds Jasper's sarcasm to be more and more endearing by the minute. It kept him going and continues to bring a smile to his face.

Before the window to respond passes by, Jack quickly retorts.

"Time is an abstract concept, but our destination should be fixed"

He is pleased at managing a comeback before the opportunity had passed, which was proving to be more and more difficult when pitted against an opponent as formidable as Jasper.

Their quirky exchanges along the journey did however make him wonder if the cat really could be a little deviant leading him astray. Whatever else she might be, Jack could certainly say that she is disciplined. Jasper was the first cat that he had ever seen pass by smaller animals without so much as a double take at the little critters.

'It could be a sign of no killer instinct... or some evolved killer instinct!'

The two continue their travel, with Jack taking in the sights which the woods have to offer, until suddenly his wandering mind snaps to attention when he notices Jasper sitting in the path facing him.

She maintains a look of significance and announces that they have arrived.

Jasper then cranes her head back over her shoulder to show him just where he has been taken to.

Jack takes a few steps in the direction shown and looks on speechless at what he finds.

Not so far away is a building which stands alone in a beautifully maintained field.

It is unlike any building he has ever seen before. The huge main section is a radiant yellow dome with a multitude of windows, and over it towers a curved cobalt hood, reaching tall into the sky and leaning over like a canopy. The building's strange shape puts Jack in mind of a crashed meteor with its trail still visible.

"What's this?" he asks with growing intrigue.

"This is where you will find your answers" Jasper replies in a sagely tone.

"What do you mean?"

"What do you mean "What do you mean?" are you a fool?" teases the cat.

"Hey, it takes one to know one. The fool answers questions while the wise question answers. I simply want to know a little more."

"Well if I'm a fool, then you had better not ask me any more questions. It's foolish to ask a "fool" for an explanation you know?"

Trying to recover the slim chance of getting information from the cat after she had used his own argument against him, Jack quickly replies with a new premise.

"But the wise ask questions, while a fool pretends to have the answers. I don't have the answer here, and I don't pretend to, so I'm asking you."

"I wouldn't want to be a fool answering questions" declares Jasper in a verbal checkmate.

Welcome

Both Jack and little Jasper enter the sphere, and the building's inviting aroma which gives it a welcoming vibe is the first thing Jack notices.

Natural light pours in through the many windows, reflecting round colourful walls, reaching up to illuminate the high ceilings. To Jack, the inside looks like an elaborate art gallery with the stunning array of strange shapes and colours, all lit up by the radiant beams of sunshine flooding in through the windows.

"Congratulations!" he hears a nurturing woman's voice call over.

He looks over to find a tall lady with short amber hair at the other side of the large hall.

She smiles and waves to him, as she gently making her way through the brightness of the room.

Jack observes the light blue clothes that she wears, similar to the ones he was in now, the kind he would expect to find medical staff clothed in.

The lady makes eye contact when she reaches him and smiles.

"Hi there, my name is Gela and welcome to the Hub."

"His name is Jack" interjects Jasper.

The woman kindly nods, acknowledging his furry companion.

'So I'm not the only one who can hear this cat talking' he thinks, somewhat relieved that his conversations with Jasper were not imagined.

13

"Wow, after all you've been through! You must have a strong identity if you still remember your name" says Gela.

"Been through?" repeats Jack with a puzzled expression.

Gela smiles at him compassionately "It's okay, I'm a nurse and I'm here to tell you everything you need to know".

She extends an open hand for him to take.

A second goes by in the reception, while a much longer time passes in his mind, as he looks to the nurse's invitation.

Normally he would have never taken the hand of a person who he had never met before, not even a nurse, but here and now he feels at peace, like he and Gela had known each other for a long time.

He decides to take the nurse's hand, and together they make their way down a corridor on the ground floor, though not before little Jasper jumps up onto his shoulder to accompany them.

"Wow you're honoured! This little troublemaker has never done that before" comments the nurse.

She then proceeds to guide Jack and his new feline friend, round the dome shaped building referred to as 'The Hub".

As they walk, Gela explains to him that the Hub is a community centre which serves as a school, primarily for children, but also for "newcomers" like Jack.

'"Newcomer"? I know I'm new here, but I seem to already have a label. And what makes us "newcomers" need school like children?'

The friendly nurse continues to talk away until he finally cuts in and asks "So

14

what is a newcomer?" curious about what makes him one, while feeling comfortable enough to voice his question.

With a smile which shows that she was hoping he would ask this, the nurse in an upbeat voice answers.

"Newcomers are the people who I'm here to help".

She then slows her tempo.

Jack instinctively braces himself, as nothing positive is ever said after someone slows down to become serious.

"This may come as a shock to you" she tells him, while tentatively placing a firm yet gentle hand on his upper arm. Then looking him straight in the eye, no longer pulling any punches, the nurse tells him.

"A newcomer is someone who has been newly reincarnated".

'Reincarnated?'

Jack's mood immediately drops and he becomes convinced that he is being made fun of, with his sceptical side prevailing as he begins to take offense.

"Am I not a little old for a new-born?" he quizzes, a question asked with a hint of spite as he decides to mock Gela's farfetched claim. Being lied to had always been a pet peeve of Jack's.

"Yes, you are old for a new-born" the nurse answers frankly "But you're actually quite young for a newcomer".

The nurse gives him a moment to process her answer before continuing.

"I know about the world you lived in, and you will be happy to know that we have come a long way since then."

15

'*She seems so sincere about this.*'

"We're living thousands of years from that time, and civilisation has made a great many strides since those barbaric ages."

'*Aren't I the lucky one?*' he sarcastically thinks to himself in introverted reply.

Jack had never liked the world in which he lived, it was so bleak and corrupt. Always he would wish for the very things that the nurse was now telling him, but was she only telling him what he wanted to hear? The extraordinary nature of her words alone were reason enough to reject what is being said. Still he listens.

"Humanity has learned a great deal about ourselves and the world we live in. Over time, our scientists and sages have found that people can indeed live again

"It is believed that people could always be born again, as a child that is. But there are also two other ways of being brought back that we now know of. The first way to come back, is to be summoned back into the material world by the sages. A feat that's been made possible by our new level of consciousness and understanding."

Jack looks to little Jasper on his shoulder, hoping for some clues, however he finds the cat is paying serious attention to what is being said.

'*That's right, look to a talking cat for clarity*' he tells himself with a sardonic smirk.

"The other way to come back, is through the will of Gaia, the Earth itself."

16

Gela then places her free hand on his other arm, to stand face to face as she tells him.

"This is how you have come back. The world we live in has chosen you to live here and now. You Jack, your consciousness and your being, has been brought back for a reason."

Hearing this does make Jack feel a little special. Gela seems so genuine to him, her eyes even watered a little when she told him this amazing news. But logic tells doubting-Jack to believe otherwise.

Feeling uncomfortable about what is being said, yet all the while being drawn in by his own curiosity, he asks "So where did I come from?" He was even beginning to like the idea of having a purpose.

He had heard stories of many elaborate hoaxes and awaited Gela's response, expecting this to all have been a prank from the tall lady with the chic lion's mane in scrubs.

"No-one knows how the Earth recreates you. All we know is that you emerge from the fountain of life" she answers.

Jack becomes weary from hearing this and little Jasper jumps down from his shoulder when he turns away for some space.

Unsure of what to do next, and beginning to feel a little lightheaded, he leans forward against the nearest wall with both hands out to support him.

'What to make of all this? It's an obvious prank, but I've nowhere to run to. What do I do?'

He looks up to the wall he is leaning on and finds a mirror on front of him,

17

but what he sees in this mirror makes his narrative come to a stop.

Within the reflection is a new face looking back.

Butterflies scatter through the pit of Jack's stomach and everything but the reflection disappears from his mind.

'No way!'

There had been times when he had looked into a mirror only to find a sad person, even a crazed person, staring back at him. But here and now the individual looking back at him from this reflection, is indeed a Jack who is undeniably the same person, yet different at the same time.

It is still his own face looking back from the mirror, there was no mistaking this. But there are also some changes.

His face is now a little more squared, with his nose and cheekbones slightly more defined. His skin itself looks much healthier now with more colour, and the iris of his eyes are a little darker. All very different, yet so familiar, but without any doubt he knows that he is indeed looking back into his own two eyes.

Flashbacks of water suddenly come flooding over Jack, as he remembers walking shin deep out of the purest water then out into the forest where Jasper had discovered him. There are notions of sound and colour inside a cave, a vastness of sensation, however the memory escapes him as quickly as it had arrived.

His eyes begin to tear up as he turns round to face Gela and Jasper once more.

Contrary to the tears of pain which were the only tears Jack had ever known, these tears do not come from the sting of the physical or verbal. Emotionally, what makes him cry now, is the overwhelming torrent of memories which embody his life. Every moment he has lived, all that he has ever experienced, everything he has ever believed in, loved, the good times and the bad. All that has ever meant anything to Jack, comes rushing back into him in this single point in time, stirring emotions that he had not felt since he was a little boy.

Gela on the other hand had seen this before. Right now Jack is mourning himself at an emotional level, even though he is not consciously aware of it, his own mind is pining for all the unfulfilled potential of his lost life.

After a good think he gathers himself and considers that he may well be living in a better world now. If there was another possibility he would like to hear it, and if things really are as Gela has described, then it would mean that everything he has ever wished for had finally come true.

Jack casts away his stand-off demeanour and looks back to the nurse with a longing need in his eyes.

"Please tell me more."

Hey

With little Jasper on his shoulder, Jack continues to ask nurse Gela questions as they make their way down the many corridors of the Hub.

"So if someone doesn't enjoy life, they can just end it and start again?"

"No" Gela answers firmly "The sages have found that gratitude plays a huge role in your reincarnation. To discard this life for the next one is the greatest insult to Gaia, one which could see you gone forever."

They reach the other side of the corridor after this answer, and the nurse takes him and his furry companion into a spacious room where two boys, both in their late teens like Jack, stand talking to each other.

Both look very athletic. One of the boys is tall and pale, with dark close-cropped hair and a very friendly smile. The other boy is shorter, with ebony skin and a pony tail of fine dreadlocks, and much like Jack this boy wears an expression which gives away nothing.

They both turn their attention to Jack's party as they enter.

At first nothing is said, but their welcoming demeanour does put the newcomer at ease.

However, despite this silent greeting, Jack still stands ready to reject them before they get the chance to reject him, an old habit which he had picked up from a life of hard knocks. He generally tried not to get too attached to anyone, even when rejection was not immediate, as the people he met would often go off in a different direction in life, one which would leave him alone in the end.

"Another one!" the tall boy exclaims, breaking the silence with a vigorous declaration which matched his strong physique.

The boy with dreadlocks nods to Jack and asks "How's it going?"

"Good thank you" he answers, unsure of what is going on but responding politely all the same.

He turns to Gela, who smiles to him reassuringly before addressing the other boys.

"This is Jack, and his friend Jasper" she tells them.

She then indicates to the tall boy "This is Thyn, he also works here at the Hub."

Thyn gives Jack a friendly wave.

Gela then indicates to the boy with the dreadlocks.

"And this is Wey. Wey has appeared today like you, he is a fellow newcomer".

Immediately this draws the attention of both so called newcomers, who look to each other in mesmerised curiosity, each growing more and more eager to know the other's story.

"Hey! When you from?" asks Jack, feeling very savvy for asking 'when' and not 'where'.

Wey, looking a little sheepish, replied that he does not know in a reluctant manner.

Gela notices Wey's discomfort, so steps in to explain.

"Although people are still the same person when they emerge from the fountain, most don't have memories from their old life".

In an upbeat voice, Thyn says "Everything you need to know is right here man".

He then guides Wey over to Jack and puts a hand on each boy's shoulder as he speaks.

"Look into each other, and not just at each other" he tells them, which makes Jack even more uncomfortable.

The thought of staring a complete stranger in the eyes whilst standing only one pace away made him very uneasy, especially when he had yet to form an opinion of said stranger. However, he could tell that Wey felt the same, so reasons that they are both in the same boat and there is nothing to lose.

Both boys make eye contact. Awkward eye contact at first.

"See the person, not just the surface, and everything important will be revealed" Thyn smoothly instructs, his voice still upbeat.

Jack lets go of his apprehension, shrugging the weight of trepidation from his shoulders to focus on "looking inside", and when he does, the eye contact becomes something more.

Both newcomers begin to see past the physical, expanding their views to take in everything around their partner as they do.

The sensation from doing this is strange to them both, as if they are both looking into one another's soul, experiencing glimpses of the other's past life, and not just metaphorically.

The sensation expands to create a world that is exclusive to the two newcomers and amidst the kaleidoscope of sound, colour and touch within their connection, Jack begins to see notions of Wey through a red mist, which would appear to be the colour of Wey's being.

From witnessing this he gains a familiarity with his fellow newcomer, as if he now knew him personally.

He sees Wey as a small child, then as a teenager, all through the red mist. It is a scattered timeline of who he is and what defines him. There are no details, but he learns all there is to know about his fellow newcomer.

Wey is stubborn, it makes him unpopular... he will stand up against anything he sees as wrong... he will always look out for the people he cares for...

Jack learns the essentials of Wey's entire story in a matter of seconds, and finds they have a lot common.

After a minute he decides to break the silence.

"Thyn gave you the name "Wey", because you kept saying "no way" when he was telling you about this new world. You're a hard worker, and you stand by your friends through thick and thin."

Wey nods knowingly, and with a friendly expression replies.

"And you Jack, you're a dreamer. Your ideals have made you an outsider, but you're a champion of your beliefs and you're true to all."

The two smile to one another, having learnt so much about their counterpart in just an instant.

23

Jasper jumps off of Jack's shoulder as both boys step forward to embrace each other as good friends.

'How can anyone be this close at meeting for the first time?' he wonders, all the while glad that this is the way things are now.

He had lived the healthiest lifestyle he possibly could have in his old life, had even stayed out of trouble, which was a rare thing where he was from. But all that good karma had ever given him was social exclusion. Now though, things are different. He can see it in Wey and can feel it in the others.

After their moment, the newcomers turn to face Gela and Thyn. They both look to their teachers to see their auras, though without sharing a connection like Jack and Wey just had. They see who the teachers are, only from the outside. It is much like viewing the other side of the sea through binoculars; they do not know what Gela and Thyn's stories are, they cannot see their aura-colours, but they can see what defines the two people on front of them.

Wey points to Thyn.

"You're a fun-loving guy who's always there to lend a hand. You're also popular with the ladies, but you're still waiting for that special one."

Thyn gives him a thumbs up and chuckles "Too much information dude."

Jack then looks to Gela and tells her.

"You're a very creative person. You're also very sensitive, so sensitive in fact, that you've found your passion in guiding newcomers".

Gela smiles as she nods "Bravo you two! You're way ahead of most

24

newcomers on their first day."

Jack and Wey look to each other with encouraging smiles, an unspoken kudos strengthening their bond.

"Now let's see how good your field work is!" Thyn chimes in.

"Field work?" they ask.

Gela rolls her eyes at Thyn, all the while smiling.

"Thyn loves the fields."

Field Work

In the middle of a field where the crops bloom in abundance, and the air carries along the sweet sound of the sun, Gela tells the boys that "By *"field work"*, Thyn really did mean "field work"".

Her short amber hair sways in the gentle breeze, while Jack and Wey look on at the rows of plants and soil that extend far over the hills under the beautiful orange sky.

"The field is my domain!" Thyn proudly chimes-in, comically thumping his chest and raising both hands as if a crowd were cheering him on.

"So why are we here?" asks Wey.

Thyn gives the newcomer a comically shocked expression, as if he had just been struck with a ridiculous question.

"Everyone should know how to grow food man. You need to know!" he declares, playfully feigning outrage at the notion of someone not knowing.

"Can't we just hunt our food?" responds Wey.

Thyn goes uncharacteristically quiet at this new question. His eyes give away how startling the newcomer's words are to him and he looks to Gela for support.

The nurse kindly steps in to explain.

"Eating animals is no longer accepted Wey" she tells the newcomer.

"Yeah man!" adds Thyn "Humans did, what they had to, to survive in the ice age and stuff, but now we're evolved man."

He strikes another grand pose after boasting about how evolved humans are now, then continues in a more serious tone.

"We don't eat animals, because we don't have to. There's some rare, and I mean RARE, circumstances where someone has actually had to eat a dead animal to survive. But it's never became the rule, and I've never met anyone who has actually had to do it."

This food for thought unsettles Jack somewhat, as almost everything he had eaten back in his old life had been meat.

'I didn't like that an animal had to die so that I could live, but it was them or me. Wasn't it?'

Thinking back on it, all of the vegetarians he saw through television programming were portrayed as weaklings, would he be able to cope? Then again, how often was the TV truthful?

"I won't complain so long as there's steady food for me" Wey resolves.

"There's an abundance for all my man! And I'm told by our newcomers that the food now is way better than it was before" replies Thyn, having regained his carefree demeanour.

Jack also resolves to find this acceptable.

'Who could complain over a steady supply of good food?'

A calmness follows this simple question, and the four in the fields quickly become more relaxed over the topic. It gives the new guys some time to digest how things are now.

27

However, the quiet that follows Thyn's words, also gives Jack's enquiring brain the space it needs to go further, making him prospect the many new possibilities of this world.

'No one eats meat? An abundance for all? Better than before?'

With so many questions to choose from, and so much to learn, he decides to start off with a broad question which may answer more than one of the volumes congregating in his eager mind.

Wondering if food is now abundant because the population was low, he goes ahead and asks what the world's population is now, becoming thrilled at learning how his old time had eventually turned out.

Going by Thyn's expression, this would appear to be a question that is often asked by newcomers, and the quirky mentor wastes no time responding to it.

"There's no exact number my man. We're all too busy to go round counting everyone. But what I can tell you is that the population now, is much higher than the populations from your time, and Wey's, put together."

'What!'

Both newcomers find this astounding, especially Jack, who had gone hungry on many occasions in his previous life. Food had always seemed so scarce in that time, so expensive and out of reach on the supermarket shelves, which leads him to even more questions about this new world.

"What country is this?" he asks. A question which also perks the curiosities of Wey.

"Well the town we're in is called Larutan" answers Thyn "But if you're wanting to know what nation this is, then think again! Those kind of countries don't exist anymore, there's only one world."

Jack and Wey go on to spend the entire afternoon bombarding Thyn and Gela with a plethora of questions about the new world they had found themselves in. And in between those questions, the boys learned first-hand about how to grow organic food in the fields.

Little Jasper had run off the minute work had begun, but the four were sure that she would return just as soon as their work was over.

At first Jack and Wey had started out with typical tourist questions like *"can you drink the water?"* They learned many of the basics of this new society, like the rarity of newcomers as the majority of people in this world, including Gela and Thyn, are born and raised by parents. But as the day progressed, so too did their questions, which became more and more philosophical.

"I like that the whole *'them and us'* turf thing is gone" says Wey, addressing Gela in an even tone while readying a bed of soil for seeds "But who keeps the peace and sorts out the bad guys?"

This was an easy one for the nurse to answer, while she was planting a round white bulb in the soil before her.

"There are no bad guys Wey. We all keep the peace and support each other."

"But what about police?" he persists.

"There are no police. Or army" she answers "We live in a world built on harmony. Crime doesn't exist anymore because no one lives in want. I suppose we're all the police in way because we all look out for one another, but formal policing is a thing of the past".

Both Wey and Jack look over to each other quietly, both processing yet another outlandish revelation.

A world built on everyone's consent had always been a dream of Jack's, now he was finally living in it.

'This world just keeps getting better and better' he thinks to himself as he waters a bed of seeds in the rich daylight *'It's all too good to be true...'*

Sure that he is about to find the proverbial fly in the ointment, Jack goes ahead and asks another question, one which could see the ruin of the nice image he presently has of this world.

"So who decides the rules for everyone?"

Not even having to think about the answer, Thyn replies.

"Why complicate things man? We're all individuals who choose to live with each other. We know what's good and bad without being told, and there's no greed, so there's no need for rules."

He smiles, then adds "Plus, the idea of the wheel would have never taken off if the cavemen had lawyers!"

Jack and Wey couldn't help but laugh at the simple brilliance of his answer, it was so true. Thyn too was getting a kick out of answering their newcomer questions.

Once Jack's laughter had subsided, he thinks some more about what Thyn had just told them.

'*Greed doesn't exist anymore?*'

Considering these words immediately brings him to his next question.

"There's no money?" he asks, stupefied, as his former society had revolved entirely around currency.

"Yeah man! Money was just pretend numbers that made weak people do bad things. But without it; the food still grows, the water still flows and the land under our feet is still here. People are happier too".

'*So civilisation no longer believes in that papermoon...*'

He and Wey look to each other again, both nodding their approval of how much sense this new world is making, then suddenly a horn sounds from the Hub in the distance.

At this Gela downs her tools and announces that dinner is ready, signalling for the boys to stop working and come eat.

"Another time!" Thyn says excitedly, a new smile beaming brightly from his bold face.

Gela closes her eyes and nods approvingly of her enthusiastic friend.

He turns his attention back to his newcomer friends, who were both visibly radiant after their first day of work in the lush fragrances of nature.

"Been great hanging out with you guys, and I look forward to seeing you tomorrow, but right now... I gotta fly!"

Thyn immediately dashes off to his new adventure, running with the energy of a young pup chasing after their favourite ball.

"So what's for dinner?" asks Wey, watching Thyn disappear into the distance.

"We'll need to see what Yendo has made for us tonight" answers Gela.

"Yendo the food man eh? Can't wait to meet him!"

The nurse and his fellow newcomer begin to make their way back to the Hub, however Jack remains standing, lost in a world of thought.

Gela looks back to notice him just standing there, looking down. She sends Wey on ahead, while wondering how Jack who had been so upbeat only a moment ago, could have become so grave all of a sudden.

She walks over to him, which the boy does not notice until he feels her gentle hand upon his shoulder.

"What's wrong Jack?" she asks him.

It had been an overwhelming day learning so many new things. Now the culture shock of living in this beautiful paradise had finally caught up with him.

"Things weren't this nice in my old time" he replies in a timid voice, not entirely sure of how to put his emotions into words.

His speech begins to quiver as he continues.

"It's all so much to take in. Why are you so nice? You don't even know me."

He asks this question with his sceptical side creeping in from the shadowy recesses of his mind, just as it often would to remind him of how selfish people can be.

Recognising what he is going through, Gela gives the newcomer a big reassuring smile.

"My purpose here is to help you Jack. We don't have the problems that you had back in your old time, but we still have our fair share. We work to master our callings, and we help each other when it is needed. There's no ulterior motive here. Everyone has a place in this world, and by helping you, I'm helping society and gaining a friend."

In the hope of comforting the newcomer, she puts her arms round the lost boy in a gentle embrace, and against her better judgment, Gela allows Jack to connect with her as he had done earlier with Wey.

A mist of colour engulfs Jack's vision, and within the purple aura of the connection which he now shares with Gela, he understands immediately that he can trust her.

She is indeed the kind woman who is here to help him, and life here; though free from conflict, still has its challenges.

Their connection lasts forever in a moment.

Upon leaving their joined aura, Jack looks into Gela's jade-green eyes with a new understanding of himself and of the world he now lives in.

He realises that she and Thyn had avoided connecting with the newcomers to spare overwhelming them on this first day.

Nevertheless, he is glad that she had chosen to end his torment here and now with this lesson from her pure aura.

With Jack consoled, the two head back to the Hub, both wearing modest smiles, which would appear to be the fashion in Larutan, a statement that shows the strength and poise of a person's character.

The Hall

Jack and Gela arrive back at the Hub to find Wey fervently talking away to a robust man in the foyer. The man smiles placidly as he patiently listens to the newcomer's enthusiastic questions and ideas, which come at him a-mile-a-minute.

"Hey Jack!" Wey calls over, waving as soon as he notices his friends arrive.

Immediately he hurries to take Jack over to meet the person to whom he had been talking, much like a toddler wanting to show an adult their new drawing.

"Jack this is Yendo! And Yendo, this is Jack!"

'Awkward...'

The two exchange their greetings, then the tank-like Yendo, perhaps in his fifties, explains that like Gela and Thyn, he too is a teacher to newcomers, and also the Hub's cook and sensei.

Yendo, who Wey had certainly taken a shine to, comes across as a very composed man to Jack, with a natural skill for pacifying those around him with how he carries himself.

Wey continues to talk away about his plans and ideas until Gela finally steps in to say

"Let's eat."

The newcomers are delighted to find that dinner at the Hub is a limitless helping of food, served in an unexpectedly large room known to the diners there as "The Hall".

'The names aren't very extravagant are they?'

However, what lacks in title in this new world, more than compensates with substance.

There must have been hundreds of people sitting round the room's many large tables, all of them bright eyed and healthy, and as large as the diners were in number, the venue's magnificence in size made them appear so much smaller than they actually were, which Jack was glad of, as the noisy cluster of an overcrowded room often made him ill at ease.

'It sure would be very difficult to crowd out a room as grand as this.'

He also notices the absence of alcohol, which also makes the night more comfortable for the newcomer.

Enjoying the flow of conversation with all the interesting people around him, Jack savours in the exciting tastes of the sweet new foods, at a table with Gela and Wey to either side of him and little Jasper at his feet.

To the other side of Gela is the plump and happy Miggles, a very talkative boy who is more of a young adult than a teenager, and though he is a little older than Jack, he comes across as very innocent as he does his best to make friends with the newcomers which makes Jack take an instant liking to him.

Also at their table are the non-identical twins Mantha and Oclea, both a little older than Miggles and a lot more mature, even with their contrasting hot and cold personalities.

Jack jovially dubs them "The Tortie-Twins" due to their remarkable hair colours that remind him of the tortie-cats that used to live with his gran.

Mantha's long auburn hair has flecks of black and white through it, while Oclea's shorter hair is mainly black with streaks of white and bronze.

Jack finds the outgoing botanist, Mantha, to be a very warm person as she uses her hands while talking away to those around her, while Oclea, the twin with gorgeous eyes, is much quieter character. Jack finds Oclea, who is a nurse to children, to be a lovable rogue on first impression, mainly due to her sense of humour along with the devilish smile she wears.

The twins' hair intrigues him so much that he goes ahead and asks what made them choose their exotic colours.

The two blush and chuckle at the interest, until they tell him that they both have their natural colours.

Evidently hair had evolved along with society during the millennias which passed while he was away.

Lastly at their section of the table is the wheelchair bound Pat, an outgoing man of around Yendo's age, who between dishing out witticisms and wolfing down food, informs the newcomers that he had been paralysed from the waist down in an accident last year, but expects to make a full recovery soon.

Dinner proves to be a very enjoyable experience for all, and a new social concept for Jack, who always regarded dining as just a necessity for refuelling and nothing more. However now he can see the social side to eating that had always eluded him until tonight. The night where he had found good friends who did not bring him reputation, status nor riches, but something far more important, contentment.

Once dinner had ran its course, Jack privately shares with Wey that he used to believe eating animals was fine, animals would eat other animals after all, but now that was changing after such fine animal free food. He is relieved to learn that Wey shared the same old and new opinions. To not be alone in this was very reassuring.

Out of habit Jack takes the notion for something sweet after dinner, then realises a lack of deserts.

Deciding to voice his palate's desires, he asks where all the deserts are.

Unfortunately the reply to the newcomer's question is a blank look from the people around him, which makes him a little uneasy.

So he elaborates.

"You know; chocolate, sugar…"

"Oh there's no need for that kind of confectionary anymore" answers Gela, wearing an understanding expression.

"Life itself is sweet now. Plus that stuff was just another "opium" from the past."

'No sweets! How will I get by?' Jack thinks to himself. He then reasons that asking himself this may indicate a habit, perhaps even an addiction. Maybe he was better off without that stuff.

'Come to think of it, it was always cheap and readily available.'

Carefree Pat notices Jack's taste for the "here and now", so turns to the newcomer with his devil-may-care grin and says "Maybe you can join me and Thyn when I get back into streaming".

Jack had never heard of streaming before, but before he gets the chance to ask what it is, Gela interrupts them and tells the newcomers that they should rest up after such a big day.

Pat quirkily feigns sheepishness at the nurse's interjection, as she ushers Jack and Wey out of the Hall, accompanied by little Jasper who follows closely behind them as everyone else tidied away the tables.

Once out of the Hall and down the corridor which takes them back to the Hub's reception, Gela stops the boys to ask if they had enjoyed their day.

Without hesitation the two tell her that they had had a wonderful time. It really was an enjoyable first day of learning, good work, and socialising.

"That's great!" says Gela, it was always so rewarding for her to hear that her newcomers had enjoyed a successful first day.

After sharing how pleased she is for them, the nurse then takes a slightly more serious air, as if building up to gruelling business.

Making a start, she says to them.

"Well you have learned a few of the basics of our society, and met some of our people..."

She then looks to them both, pausing with heartfelt anticipation before carrying on.

"As you know, our culture is one built on consent, and it is very early days yet, but I must ask each of you... would you like to be part of this society?"

Both Jack and Wey look to each other with a puzzled expression.

Neither boy had ever been asked a question even remotely like this before, they had never even considered a question like this existed.

However, here and now the boys had been asked it.

They both communicate to each other through eye contact alone, and as they do a smile begins to grow across each boy's face.

When their unspoken dialogue finishes, they both turn back to face Gela and answer the same.

"Yes!"

They had already begun to fit into life here in Larutan after all.

Relief washes over Gela.

She had never received a "no" before, but one should never become complacent as there could always be a first time.

Jack does step in however, comically waving his finger to add a more serious point.

"But I will withdraw my consent, should I learn that anything here is not what I am lead to believe it is."

"That's no problem Jack" answers the nurse with a heartening smile.

"Yeah, what Jack said. By the way, what would have happened if we had said no?" asks Wey, never shying away from an awkward question.

This amuses Gela, as she has now come to expect this sort of thing from him.

"If that were the case Wey, we would have done our best to accommodate you, while respecting your wishes. It has never happened before, but it is important for a society to let people live free and make their own decisions."

"What happens now that we have consented?" asks Jack, being more to the point.

"Now that you have consented, I can help you find your place here. Do more days like today sound good to you?"

Both boys nod in reply.

"Great, we can get started tomorrow. Now it's time for you to get some rest, I'll show you to the accommodation we have available, that is if you're happy to stay here at the Hub?"

The newcomers are fine with these living arrangements, and on a lighter note, Gela informs them that the rooms would still have been offered tonight, even if they had declined a place in this society.

She takes both boys up to the Hub's first floor and shows them to their new, yet comforting, abodes.

Each private dwelling is an intricate network of rooms and extensions, including a large bedroom, washroom, and their very own kitchen. Jack finds

41

the high-ceilinged apartments to be "rubik cube" like in appearance, but what impresses him most about his new room, is how fresh it is. It was as if it had known nothing but care while awaiting him to become its first inhabitant.

Each apartment also offers a beautiful view of the very forest from which both boys had emerged.

Jack and Wey, who are now next door neighbours, are both very impressed.

Wey is the first to retire, wishing both Jack and Gela a good night before going to his room.

Jack is also worn out from such a big day, but still can't help but smile while reflecting back on how wonderful it had been.

He opens the door to his accommodation, with little Jasper racing in ahead of him, then realises that the door has no lock.

Immediately he turns to Gela and asks why this is.

The nurse smiles reassuringly and tells him "Times are safe now, locks haven't been used for centuries."

'No locks?'

Normally Jack would have never stepped into an unfamiliar room and slept there without a lock. EVER. However, after connecting with Gela earlier, he understands that it truly is safe now. All the same he did plan on keeping something heavy on front of the door for his own peace of mind, for though he knows for a fact the world is now safe, his old instincts are still alive and kicking, and they always advise caution.

He takes in the room's fresh sandalwood scent through the open door while looking straight out onto the forest's soothing view.

The trees reach tall as they stretch out to blissfully brush the clouds in the swaying breeze. It is a welcoming sight, and the sight coupled with the room's fine scent, makes Jack truly feel at home.

Taking in the view also reminds him of a question, one which was so obvious that both he and Wey had forgotten to ask it when in the fields today.

With his quizzical cap back on, he looks the nurse in her kind jade eyes and asks her why the sky is orange.

As ideal as the world is now, he does wish that the sky was that peaceful shade of blue he remembered seeing as a child. He had never seen enough of that gorgeous sky in his old life.

With a sigh, Gela explains.

"I'm afraid that's part of our heritage. Pollution from your time and the centuries that followed, made our sky go from blue to orange. Now we live with a new colour of day".

A forlorn expression devastates Jack's face upon hearing these words. The world would have been perfect were it not for this.

Noticing his longing expression, Gela explains.

"We have recovered most of the world. Our roads and our buildings, including this one, are made from the debris that once filled our oceans. The air and the water were almost finished, but now they thrive beautifully and support life again."

Then looking over to the sky, she adds.

"The colour of the sky can be good thing or bad one, depending on what you make of it. And if it is still an eyesore to you, then it may comfort you to know that our scientists and sages are working on a way to heal this remaining scar."

Jack looks through the window and out into the evening.

'*So there are people out there working on a way to bring back my blue sky...*'

This slim element of hope is all he needs to rest easy tonight.

The two bid each other a good night and he enters his new room, securing his door, then Jack immediately lies down on the bed next to Jasper, falling asleep the minute his head hits the pillow.

A New Day

Stirring from his sleep at first light, Jack rises immediately from the fresh new bed in which he had spent his first night, and walks over to look out from his new bedroom window.

With a deep inhalation of the clear Larutan air, savouring the morning as it pours in brightening his face, Jack looks out to all the beauty which bides within the limitless possibilities awaiting outside, and smiles.

'Today truly is the first day of the rest of my life.'

In the bathroom he discovers a fascinating new type of shower, one which uses light and sound as well as water to clean its occupant.

After washing himself with the organic oils and vinegars which the people of this time evidently use to clean themselves with, he puts on some of the new scented clothes which hang in his wardrobe.

Once dressed, he quickly goes off to explore the Hub, leaving his little friend Jasper to continue her beauty sleep.

From traveling through the Hub's many corridors and seeing more of its large open rooms, Jack realises just how big the place actually is; much larger than it looked from the outside.

Eventually his exploration takes him to the very same hall where he had dined last night, and in it he finds Yendo drinking tea at a small table near the kitchen.

"Hi there Jack" the chef's strong voice calls over to him in a welcoming tone.

"Hi" Jack replies, doing his best to contain the excitement over what this new day may bring.

"How do you feel after your first day out in the fields?"

"Great! I had a brilliant day yesterday, the food was great too!"

"Glad to hear it."

The large man pauses for a moment, then after quick consideration, asks.

"How would you like to help out in the kitchen before the rest get up for breakfast?"

Jack eagerly agrees, thrilled at having the chance to contribute to the magic of this new place he discovered yesterday. But once Yendo leads him into the kitchen, he realises that he does not know the first thing about kitchen work.

Negative thoughts swarm his mind from the embarrassment of such fool-hardy naivety. His embarrassment continues to grow and grow, and though barely a second had passed, he knows that it will go on forever, that is until Yendo lays a hand on his shoulder.

He looks up to the chef, who offers a reassuring expression and tells him.

"Don't worry. I'll show you everything you need to know."

It turns out that Jack is made for kitchen work.

Learning about the exciting new foods and preparing them for everyone, proves to be a very rewarding endeavour for the newcomer.

"There's something about working with your own hands!" he calls over to Yendo while finely slicing a green squash.

"Every job in my old time seemed to be selling stuff that people didn't want."

"Yep" the chef agrees, as he fills a giant pot with water.

"There's nothing like doing something real with your own two hands. Speaking of which; you're knife skills are very impressive, where you a chef in your old life?"

"No. I just figured it ought to be done properly" answers a flattered Jack.

Yendo looks over to him fondly and nods.

With a successful breakfast service under his belt, the patrons of the Hall congratulate Jack on his triumphant foray in the kitchen on their way out, before he is re-joined by little Jasper.

After everyone had left, Yendo takes Jack and Jasper, along with Wey who had also waited behind, to yet another part of the Hub.

The newcomers soon find themselves standing with Yendo before a considerably large set of double-doors. The large chef wastes no time in throwing them open to reveal what awaits inside, announcing.

"This here is the dojo."

'Dojo?'

The name immediately draws the attention of both boys.

It is a fairly large room, not quite as large as the Hall they had dined in, but far more fascinating.

The wooden floor is decked out with plants and wooden apparatus, and the boys see a low platform of large stone tiles at the centre.

"Take a look around if you like."

Jasper wastes no time in running off to explore, while the newcomers proceed at a more tentative pace.

Jack comes across a man-sized wooden tower with straight arms protruding from the sturdy body. It reminds him of films he had seen in his previous life, the ones where the kung-fu experts would quickly box a similar type of tower, only this one also had small scratch marks which look as though they had been made by animals.

"So what happens in here" asks Wey.

"I see what looks like weapons, but there's plants and flowers too."

"Correct Wey. Those sticks you see would have been used as weapons in your old time, but the essence of a martial art is to compose oneself, and improve your connection with the world. We still use these weapons in the fighting styles from ages past, but not to become warriors. We harness them as an extension of ourselves, to better connect with the world around us."

Yendo then gestures at one of the flower pots.

"We also understand the world better when we grow these plants".

Both boys are riveted to the teacher's words, eager to know why the plants in here would help them better understand the world, and with keen interest Jack enquires.

"What do we learn from plants in here that we don't learn from growing them in the fields?"

Sensei Yendo smiles, this clearly a question which he had hoped would be asked, and he wastes no time in answering.

"In one word Jack, we learn relationship. Out in the fields you grow the plants to eat them as soon as they're ready, but in here we don't.

"Here we make them thrive for as long as our care will allow, and from them you will learn new perspectives, like how there is energy in all things. Did you happen to see the energy in the vegetables you prepared earlier in the kitchen?"

Jack shakes his head, feeling awkward from the certainty that his answer is wrong.

Yendo notices the insecurity and explains.

"Don't worry if you didn't, there is no wrong answer here, it's all about perception. From my relationship with the plants in here, I can see the power of the food I eat. The vegetables you cut earlier today were not just a means of filling ourselves, but also a natural transfer of energy. A seed grew into something more, that is energy. The soil that nourished it, was energy. The water it absorbed, was energy. The sunlight that made it grow, was energy. The people who cared for it, then harvested it, was energy. Even you, preparing it in the kitchen today, was energy. The food we eat is so much more than we realise, and so much more becomes possible when we do realise this."

Jack had never thought of food in this way before. He could suddenly feel the energy from what he had eaten earlier, channel through his body, empowering his life-force with this new way of thinking.

Although nothing had physically changed, the world as he sees it now had done so ever so slightly. It had become a place filled with many more possibilities, which were always there waiting to be discovered.

His contemplation is cut short however when Miggles enters the dojo with an entourage of small animals.

"Hi guys!" calls Miggles.

Yendo returns the greeting as he watches the animals pour into the dojo, while planning how the newcomers first class should unfold.

'That explains the scratch marks, but why are they here?' Jack wonders, watching the little dogs, cats, pigs, and chickens play around the apparatus.

This was the first time that Jack had ever seen a pig or a chicken in real life.

They seemed overjoyed at running around, more so than the dogs, and their happy smiles where something to be cherished. From watching them he discovers that chickens also purr.

A tiny brown cat slowly walks up to the newcomer, and in a sleepy voice says.

"Hullo"

"Another talking cat! Wow!" declares an impressed Jack, who wastes no time in talking away to the little guy.

"Hi there, it's nice to meet you. My name is Jack, what's yours?"

He can tell how refined and intelligent this petite tom is just from looking at him, but instead of replying, the cat simply stares at him blankly, then again says "Hullo".

"His name is Uily" Miggles calls over, indicating the little brown cat.

Not understanding why the cat is only saying hello, the newcomer looks over to Miggles, hoping for a further explanation.

"I guess you didn't know, so here, let me explain:

"Although most mammals can talk, it is very rare for them to converse using language like humans. Cats who can talk are very rare".

"Yeah!" concurs a triumphant Jasper from atop of a nearby tower.

With an amused smile at her loftiness, Miggles continues.

"Over time humans and other mammals have learned from each other. We have taught them how to talk verbally, and they have taught us how to speak clearly without using words. I heard that you and Wey have already begun connecting, you have our animal friends to thank for that."

"I see" replies Jack, stepping forward to pet Uily on the head and begin a new friendship.

"It's time!" announces Sensei Yendo.

The dojo immediately fills with energy, and suddenly, everyone both big and small stands ready.

"Uily, I'd like you to stay where you are."

51

The cat nods, clearly understanding the sensei's instruction.

'Was it the way he said it?' Jack asks himself, wondering how a cat who could not say much was able to understand such instructions.

"And you Jack, I want you to lift Uily."

The task seemed simple enough. He wonders why he has to pick up a cat and what the following instruction would be.

Bending down with his knees to get as close to level as he possibly could with little Uily, Jack with his hands under the cat's front arms, goes to lift Uily off the ground, only to find that the little brown tom is completely immovable.

It is as if the furry-one was made of cement and glued to the floor, he just would not move.

"How is this possible?" he exclaims.

"It is called "Spirit Point"" answers Yendo, who looks over to make sure that Wey is also paying attention.

"When you relax completely, the other person doesn't have a rigid form to hold on to. When your weight is underside, the pull of gravity outweighs the pull of your opponent. And most importantly; the serenity of a disciplined mind has the will to be exactly where it wishes to be. This is GaiKiZen, and this is what I can teach you."

Eager to learn more about this powerful, yet bizarrely gentle martial art, both newcomers follow their sensei's instructions with keen interest.

Jack does not start the training meekly, nor does he enter with bravado. He simply does his best to learn whilst keeping a healthy confidence, one which eventually sees him becoming very good for a beginner.

He and his three human partners spend hours training on the tiled area in the dojo, going through all the basics, while the little pigs, chickens, cats and dogs, along with proud Jasper, run around playing throughout the surrounding apparatus.

The two newcomers, and the two more experienced martial artists, learn a lot from their opponents, blending with one another's movement to absorb attacks and gently throw each other using their attacker's own energy.

"Don't think of the physical act of throwing" instructs Yendo "Just have the feeling and the rest will come".

Miggles turns to the newcomers, and with a whisper adds.

"The feeling is my favourite part."

Jack's abilities go from strength to strength as the morning progresses. He even receives high praise from Miggles after managing an expert throw on Wey, but upon finishing the throw, Yendo immediately instructs Jack to hold still and maintain his position before he could reset his form.

The sensei then walks over to the confident newcomer, examining him, studying his posture and balance.

With a wry smile priming his next move, Sensei Yendo walks closer to Jack and blows on the static newcomer, and unfortunately for Jack, this simple gust of air from his teacher's lungs, is all it takes to knock him to the ground.

The fall also brings Jack down a peg, making him realise he still has a long way to go.

Noticing the newcomer's incorrigible positivity, Yendo explains.

"It's all vibration. The key is to always be relaxed. Be relaxed, but also be physically moving.

"Even when you're not moving, at least have the intention to move, and always keep your mind still".

The words perplex the humbled newcomer, so his sensei elaborates a little further.

"You fell just there because your body was stiff and your mind was animated. To be immovable your mind needs to be still, and your body relaxed."

The statement still makes no sense whatsoever, but Jack feels as though he understands some of it, mainly thanks to the practice in the dojo today.

'It's all very abstract'.

After more throws and rolls, both newcomers are tasked with the challenge of toppling a kneeling Miggles.

Together the two push into the top of the happy boy's shoulders, diagonally down through to the floor beneath with all their might, but try as the might, they are unable to shift their very helpful friend.

"Great Miggles, you have become much more coordinated" compliments Yendo, before clapping his hands to call an end to the exercise.

"Each of you take a jo and we'll go through the basics."

Jack finds the jo to be a well-balanced stick, very light in weight and made from the sturdiest soft wood that he has ever come by.

The newcomers find that using the jo is much like the throwing exercises they had practiced all morning: so long as you relax, keep your posture, and never tense up; your opponent, or jo, will move around you at will, without you having to make any effort at all.

It proves to be a very enjoyable experience for both the newcomers and their trainers, and Sensei Yendo calls an end to practice for today once the four finish their jo exercises.

The boys and their sensei kneel and respectfully bow to each other in an important gesture of decorum, before getting up to discover the sensation of being energised, but also relaxed, as they put the jo's away.

Upon seeing the martial artists clearing up, the little animals immediately dash over for love and affection. Jasper swiftly prizes her claim to Jack, jumping onto his shoulder before any of the others could get to him.

As Jack strokes the elegant ginger cat perched to his left, Miggles explains that the visit from the little mammals is too, part of their training.

"A person can discover who they really are from their relationship with other animals."

Jack takes a moment to consider his relationship with their visitors.

He had liked them all, and at no-disrespect to them, felt honoured that a cat as intelligent and independent as Jasper had chosen him to be "her person".

The little animals stay for as long as they feel like, which is not long before they move on to their next port of call, which would appear to be the forest.

As Uily leads the gang of little animals, with the exception of proud Jasper, out of the dojo, Jack looks to Miggles and asks why he is no longer shepherding them.

"Oh I'm no shepherd" Miggles replies diplomatically, while the pack try to cram through the doors all at once.

"The mammals are their own bosses, they only needed me to get into the dojo."

Eventually the miniature stampede breaks through, and they all run out onto their next adventure, with Uily leading the charge and a cute little pig scuttling at the tail end of the crowd.

Feeling refreshed and satisfied, the three boys thank Yendo for the class then go on for more work in the fields.

Little Jasper again runs off at the mention of work, making her person smile in his certainty that she would return when the work was over.

"I hope you can make it back in time to help me out with dinner" Yendo calls to Jack as he leaves.

"I'll be back if the fields can spare me" the newcomer calls back, giving his sensei a confident grin.

They walk out onto the pathways that lead up to the hills where the crops grow, all the while discussing the calmness and power of their martial art.

Eventually they meet up with Thyn and his team, and as they work away, the boys and Thyn continue talk about GaiKiZen with a lot of difficulty.

They have a good laugh at trying to find the correct words to describe their experiences in the dojo, which was no mean task when trying to describe an art-form with such abstract concepts.

"It's heavy, but it's also light. It's light-heavy!" says Wey.

"Sounds like gibberish to me" replies Jack, bringing about another round of laughter at yet another comical try.

After long conversations and many more failed attempts of finding the proper words, Thyn surmises.

"It's not about thinking, it's about not thinking."

A statement so ridiculous that the boys cannot help but laugh again, while at the same time agreeing that there is no better way of describing it.

Besides the hilarity of attempting to describe Ki, working outside in the fields on yet another gorgeously sunny afternoon, makes for a very fine second day for the newcomers.

As new field hands, Jack and Wey do a great job of tending to the crops, Wey even manages to keep pace with the more experienced farmers to everyone's amazement.

Jack may not have been able to match his fellow newcomer's pace, but he does find that working with the energy of nature in the pleasantly warm sun, to be a very rewarding task, one which allowed him to grow alongside the plants he tended to.

Upon reflection he realises there was no pressure in the fields or in kitchen, a stark contrast from his old time, where the adults always seemed to be stressed and harassed by their never-ending workloads with horrible bosses.

'Society really has come a long way. The people have changed. They're nice to each other now, they even enjoy their work and appreciate life'.

The newcomers' time in the fields flies in so fast that before they know it, Gela arrives to let Jack know that preparations for tonight's dinner are underway.

He receives some jesting from the other field hands at the prospect of leaving early, which was to be expected from such an outgoing crowd, but before he leaves, Jack tactfully uses his centre stage to reply openly.

"I'm having a great time here Gela, but what am I, if I don't live up to the word I gave Yendo?"

The team had wanted him to stay having enjoyed his company, but they do understand that he had made commitments, and so Jack heads back to the Hub's kitchen, with everyone in the fields including Gela, bearing a smile of great admiration for him.

With Jack walking away, his respect unquestioned, and with Wey professionally tending crops just out of earshot, Thyn turns to Miggles and asks.

"So just how good is their Ki?"

Jack is introduced to the energetic nurse Liss, a regular helper at the Hub's kitchen, when they get back to the Hub, and learns that Gela will also be helping tonight.

Together; he, Gela, Liss, and Yendo prepare a bounty of fried vegetables in a sweet lemon batter, along with tomato-dough bread, cacao-discs, and rice with pulses in a variety of exotic sauces, and before they know it, dinner preparations are completed on time as planned.

Yendo invites the outgoing Liss to sound the Hub's horn for dinner.

"With pleasure!" bellows the short nurse, in a tone which is surprisingly deep and very far from her normal tenor.

The energetic Liss then struts over to the horn, all the while making high-pitched "Woo!-Woo!" noises like the trains of old, which astonishes Jack who wonders how a person so slight in build could achieve such an impressive feat of noise.

Soon after the nurse tugs the cord which sounds the horn for dinner, the guests begin arriving and the feast promptly begins.

Jack is re-joined by Jasper the minute he and the other chefs come out of the kitchen, and tonight he sits with the same company as last night, plus the addition of Thyn.

After another evening of good food and welcome company, Thyn invites Jack and Wey to hang out with himself, Miggles and the tortie-twins.

It would appear the name "tortie-twins" had caught on.

Jack and Wey keenly accept the invitation, and after dinner the young diners set off for the forest, eventually arriving at the foot of a rocky hill known as "The Crag".

In order to gain a better view of the forest which surrounds them, the six make their way up to a higher point in the rocks, and when they get there, all six are taken by the splendour of the twilight orange sky as it fades away to a dusky pink. Jack is captivated by the illumination from the full moon as he looks on to the never-ending landscape below.

Seeing the vigour of the forest trees gets his mind going again, and he shares with Wey that there was nothing like this in his old life. A statement which is empirically true to Jack, as although the Earth did have green places back then, the world in which he had lived was entirely made from cement, at least in his experience.

"Same here" Wey replies "I don't remember much of my old life. But I do know that sights like this were a rare thing".

Both newcomers feel at peace from looking at the rich panorama before them.

The night goes by smoothly, with ample stories and laughter shared among good friends, and among the moments of laughter, joy, and peace, while little Jasper enjoyed her climb about the rocks, Jack realizes that tonight truly was the best night he has ever lived.

'Ever lived yet' he corrects himself, realising all of the great possibilities that now await him.

Later on Thyn notices movement from some nearby bushes and stands up, peering out to pinpoint exactly where it is coming from, then with an excited smile growing across his bold, energetic face he calls out "Is that who I think

60

it is?"

As these words are said, another group who are ages with Jack and his friends, emerge from the woods.

"It is!" announces an enthusiastic Thyn.

"Hey guys!" a boy from the other group calls back while approaching the Crag.

'Who is this visitor and his group?' Jack wonders. He is glad that they are wearing the same keen smiles as his group.

The boy and Thyn step forward, and with their left hand grip the other's left wrist, as if giving some kind of handshake.

"A little low down tonight are we?" jibes the visitor in a playful manner, indicating the rock level where Thyn and his friends had spent the evening. Keeping with the bravado, Thyn responds.

"We're high enough. I didn't think we'd have a visit from our neighbouring friends so soon! How long's it been, two weeks?"

"It's been too long" the boy answers with an candid smile. "Dance tonight?"

"Totally!" agrees Thyn "We'll join you up there, we have some new guys who've never seen this before."

Still wearing his friendly smile, the visitor nods and the two lock wrists again before the visiting group moves off.

'Dance? Whats happening now?' Jack thinks to himself as Thyn walks over.

"Well I have a lot to explain, and a short time to explain it. Where to start...?"

Thyn smiles at his hopeless lack of words, and looks over to Miggles for some inspiration, who offers him none.

He continues "You know how you learned about moving coordinated and effortlessly in the dojo earlier?"

"Yes" nod both newcomers.

"Well..." Thyn's words fade away as he relaxes both arms out to his sides, then calmly, millimetre by millimetre, his body lifts off the ground.

"Wow!" exclaim both Jack and Wey.

The laws of physics would appear to have changed along with society and hair colour while they had been gone.

"This is impossible!" emotes a very impressed Jack, "Where are the strings?" exclaims Wey.

"It's all very possible" replies Miggles in a level tone. "People flying is another frontier in this world you've found yourselves in. Any disciplined person can levitate, but some fearless types like Thyn here, are taking it to new levels."

"How do I learn to fly?" asks Wey eagerly.

"In time" answers Miggles, shooting down the newcomer's cavalier zest.

Upon seeing Wey's expression from Miggles curtness, Thyn decides to oblige the curious newcomer with a little more information.

"First learn to levitate man" he says, inviting both newcomers to come try, which draws concerned looks from Miggles.

"Do it over here, if you fall, it will be a safe landing."

62

Both Jack and Wey move over to where Thyn had indicated.

"Remember what you learned at GaiKiZen" instructs Thyn, and these words alone are enough to make the tranquillity of the art return to the newcomers, alleviating any tensions which they may have been carrying.

"Now focus on your spirit point and think upwards, right up, through the top of your head."

Miggles looks over to Thyn as if to say *"Is that the best you can describe it?"* Thyn raises his hands and shrugs in quiet reply.

But sure enough, and ever so slightly, both Jack and Wey begin to levitate off the ground.

At first their form is shaky, and only a hair's width from the surface, but before they know it, both newcomers are elegantly holding themselves up several feet in the air.

Magic is all around as the group pause for breath, witnessing the two newcomers achieve such great feats on their second day. A rare sight indeed.

To Jack, it feels as though he is inside an energy bubble which is expanding out from the pit of his stomach. It feels as serene as a heavenly cloud, and to him the growing bubble encircling everything encapsulates his perfect notion of peace.

Background noise begins to fade from his awareness as his energy expands, until finally all he can hear, is a continuous high-pitched whine which is very slight in volume.

The magic soon bursts however, when both boys fall back down to the ground beneath them.

Upon impact of the small crash landing, the group applaud their efforts and Jasper runs over to check that her person is unharmed.

Warmed by his little friend's concern, Jack picks up his faithful companion and gives her some grateful attention. The cat does not say a word, but without speaking they both understand each other.

"Good effort you guys!" Thyn praises "But that's it for tonight. Right now we're going to stream at the top with our friends up there."

He then raises his hands to ensure that his next point is clearly noted.

"And don't try to stream whatever you do. You need to crawl before you can run man."

"Stream?" asks Jack, recalling Pat using the same word at dinner last night.

"Streaming is the word for flying" answers Mantha as worry begins to spread across her soft features.

'So Pat's accident involved flying' thinks Jack, beginning to realise the dangers.

Miggles wades in when he notices the newcomer's mind at work.

"They call it "streaming" because in order to fly, you must be able to travel through the invisible slipstreams of energy that flow through the air. I tried it a while ago, it was fun, but the risks were too high, so I've not done it since."

'Slipstream? A form of flying that doesn't involve wings or propellers?' It

64

sounds very cool to Jack, who notices that Wey could barely contain his own excitement over the prospect of getting up there.

Mantha also notes the interest of both newcomers, so steps in with her stern warning with hand gestures to match.

"I've never tried it, because it's a stupid thing to do!"

Her eyes begin to water from the outburst, and with a few breaths she slows down before continuing.

"Look at Pat who you met at dinner. How would you feel if you were injured like him, because that's what streaming's done to Pat!"

The group go quiet after her outburst, their bravado and excitement vanishes, leaving only an uncomfortable silence which seems to last for an awkward eternity.

The silence is tense, no one dared to look up while the air was hollow with trepidation, but once the quiet had gone on for long enough in his opinion, Jack decides the time had come to end it.

He approaches Mantha, placing a tender hand on her shoulder and looking the twin kindly in the eyes. With the hope of comforting his sensitive new friend, he tells her.

"Don't worry Mantha, Wey and I can't even levitate yet, let alone fly. We will be standing next to you all night.

"I might not know what tomorrow will bring, but for tonight I can assure you that we won't try to stream."

Hearing this is a relief to Mantha who cuddles him for his kind words.

65

Jack looks over to Wey, who gives a thumbs up to show that he is on board with the promise.

Noticing the resolution, Thyn in a more sombre tone says "Let's go". He and Oclea levitate up to the top of the Crag, while the rest make their way up on foot.

The night sky is also different in this future Jack had awoken in.

Where there was once the shroud of a dark curtain laced with pinhole stars, that famous night sky which had gifted the world with many answers and even more questions, the night sky now is a jaded mist blending dark turquoise with purples and pinks.

He and the non-flyers reach the top to find Thyn fixed to a single point in the new sky, the streamer's body maintaining a perfectly straight posture as he whirls vertically backward in the spot.

Near Thyn is the visitor boy, who like him also moves whilst fixed to a single point in the sky, only the visitor spins in all directions like a gyroscope. Jack could see why Thyn referred to it a "dance".

"Hey guys!" calls Oclea from above as she abruptly whirs past them. The sound of her voice trails behind her, closely followed by two boys from the visiting group.

Jack's grounded team join the visiting non-flyers and together they all watch the five streamers glide through the night sky. To see his friends gracefully travel through the air at such high speeds proves to be something spectacular.

Wey, standing on the Crag's plateau, his gaze fixed upward and stars in his eyes says to Jack.

"It's like fireworks, only its people up there."

After many fancy manoeuvres and splendid sky play, the streamers decide to finish off the night with a race above the Crag.

Jack, noticing both Mantha and Miggles' apprehension as it's announced, takes Mantha's hand into his to comfort his friend who had shown such great worry from the beginning. The gentle twin smiles gratefully for his concern along with Miggles, before they look back to see the streamers take off.

Out of everyone in the sky, Oclea proves to have the best control in the air, while Thyn and the visitor boy lead the race neck-in-neck by a clear mile.

Thyn and the visitor boy prove to be the most skilled of the streamers, there was no doubting this, while the remaining two boys, although capable, simply could not compete at the level of the other three.

What Jack witnesses as he looks up to the wonders above is truly intense.

Thyn and the visitor boy continuously pull ahead of one another, both vying for victory as their streams break through to faster channels in the air.

Jack can see their concentration, their determination, both have become the contender who will not be beaten, but he also sees a shared respect between the two.

'Truly, healthy competition'.

Both groups in the mixed crowd below cheer for their respected leaders, and a bead of sweat begins to trickle down Jack's brow while the noise from the grounded supporters escalates.

The finish between the two draws closer, and without even realising it, Jack becomes so absorbed in the excitement that he even finds himself shouting out loud for Thyn to win.

He had never been much of a sports person before; another first in this present future.

'Thyn is going to win this! I know it!' he tells himself, believing it so strongly, as if his friend had already won.

The two leaders charge through the finish at last and the cheering escalates further.

The magnificence of it all, the elevated feeling of the crowd, the anticipation in the air, the erupting noise, makes the moment an even more special one to remember.

All the roars and shouts of encouragement finally reach their crescendo when the three remaining streamers reach the finish, and the two leaders courteously "shake" like good sportsmen.

The race was so close however that Jack could not tell who had won.

He looks around and feels at peace when he sees how happy everyone is with the outcome.

Though the good vibes are welcome to him, the newcomer is still eager to hear that Thyn had won, a truth which existed only in his mind, based solely his own hopeful instinct, until the visitor boy finally holds up Thyn's hand to officially declare the winner for their spectators.

Everyone present lets out a grand cheer from the top of the Crag, calling a great finish to a wonderful night.

"Until next time!" the visitor boy says in his high-spirited tone, while locking wrists with Thyn one last time tonight.

"Can't wait!" Thyn replies, wearing his bold smile.

Jack and his friends remain at the top of the Crag once the visiting group leave.

They spend the rest of the night chatting away about the race and whatever else is on their minds. Each give their accounts of the race, from Jack and Wey's astonishment, to Miggles' technical criticism, to Mantha's concerns, until finally they reach a point where nothing more needs to be said. Jack and his friends are so fulfilled by the night's excellence that nothing else matters. Life is but a dream.

Time Goes By

Part I

Jack settles into his new life contently, enjoying each passing day with rewarding work in the Hub's kitchen, as well as the healthy work out in the fields.

It is often said that "man is a social animal", and he had managed to come alive in ways that were new to him thanks to his new social life. Helping others with his everyday interactions and endeavours gave him new value in how he sees himself.

'The world is a lot prettier when you don't have a tv or negative people narrating what's going on.'

Being able to contribute to society by growing and preparing its food, or as he liked to romanticise; *"maintain the circle of life in this part of the world"* made all the difference to his self-esteem. Jack really enjoyed growing such great food and preparing it in the Hub's kitchen for his friends and neighbours, and despite the big impression which food had made to his life, he still spends most of his time enjoying activities outside of work.

During a typical day, before work that is, he would learn more about this society from Gela and Yendo before going on to "contribute to the community's food supply".

Later, he would regularly meet up with his friends; Wey, Thyn, Mantha,

Oclea and Miggles, to share in whatever good times they would have going. Such great friends, all heart, every one of them. The first group that Jack had ever felt content in.

Under Yendo's tuition, Jack also trains rigorously in the dojo every day with Wey, then one day at the beginning of class, both boys are approached by their sensei.

"Choose" is the only word their teacher has for them as he presents them with a variety of seeds cupped in his formidable hands.

After several lessons Jack was able to tell without any doubt, that his mountain of muscle sensei, who could overcome any obstacle using his gentle ki, was far more powerful than anyone he had ever met before. Easily more powerful than the people in his old time would even have allowed themselves to imagine. Truly an example to live up to.

The two newcomers smile in anticipation at the sight of the seeds in their sensei's cupped hands.

It was such an honour to have finally been given the privilege of personally growing their own plant in the dojo. A task which would require commitment, one which both boys are now ready for.

They step closer to see the abundant mix in their sensei's hands.

'No two are the same and there's so many!' Jack thinks to himself, pondering which one to choose.

Wey, who is much less hesitant, steps forward and chooses first. From the pile he picks a diamond shaped seed which is cobalt in colour.

71

"You have chosen a suven" announces Yendo.

Wey silently bows then steps back.

Now Jack's turn.

He quickly scans the selection in his sensei's hands, then hastily draws his own choice in an effort to hide his hesitance.

In his hand, Jack finds a relatively large green seed.

"You have chosen surta" Yendo announces.

'"Surta" wonder what this is?' he thinks, hoping that becoming the proverbial "deer caught in headlights", as they said in his old time, did not make him choose wrongly here.

He ceremoniously bows in gratitude then steps back next to Wey, with the round green seed in his hand.

The sensei shows them two plant pots, both filled with soil and tells them.

"Here is where your new friends will live. Like many before you, you may be questioning if you have made the best choice, as it was thrust upon you. Just remember that your decision has come from within, therefore it is meant to be."

The words ring very true with Jack.

"You may well have chosen your perfect match, however, if your karma here is to make a mistake, then it is up to you to take that mistake and make it grow into a relationship that harmonises. Mistakes are our best teachers, and like the best sunshine, they allow us to grow beautifully."

The words resonate with Jack, who is positive that he had chosen wrong.

72

"Do not focus on the negative" continues Yendo "It is more likely that fortune has favoured you today. Now please proceed with positive expectations, as a positive mind can expect positive outcomes."

"Thank you, Sensei!" both boys reply at audible level, before bowing to quickly to move off and plant their seeds.

Time Goes By
Part II

One day at the Hub, during his daily meeting with Gela, who today talks about their neighbouring communities and customs, Jack gets thinking, and again contrasts his present situation with the past, creating yet another question which nags away at him.

After lots of consideration he decides to ask Gela about the topic of religion, which was on his mind today, a topic which could start arguments in his old life, yet something he had still to come by here in Larutan.

After learning about the high city of Greenleaves and the scenic views from its elevated altitude, he goes ahead and asks the question which had been badgering him.

"Gela" he interrupts, before the nurse could move on to talk about the next town.

"I've not seen any sign of religion since I got here. Well besides everyone being nice to each other, which could mean very religious... or very not religious... Does it still exist?"

Expecting this to be an awkward question, he instinctively holds his breathe, bracing for the answer. You often had to be careful when talking about beliefs in his old time.

However Gela simply smiles with the same grace as she always does to his many other questions.

"Yes Jack, religion still exists. In fact there are many people in our town hold religious beliefs."

Jack had no idea. How could his friends and neighbours have religious beliefs without him knowing?

And so begins his customary routine of follow up questions.

"Then where are all the churches, and why has no one tried to get me to join one?"

The nurse smiles her ever soothing smile.

"You seem to hold a prejudiced view on religion. I noticed this on your first day, when we shared our brief connection in the fields."

She clearly said this to get him thinking, and it works.

Although Jack had discovered the essence of the kind nurse's character, he had not found anything about religion within their connection on that day. Though he had apparently shown his hand on the matter.

Examining himself, as well as the world around him, Jack begins to realise that the nurse's observation may be true.

He finds that he does indeed hold a prejudice view of religion, but righteously so in his mind.

All he thought about when reflecting on religion, was the division it created. The wars and suffering it caused, regardless of whatever good deeds some of the charitable believers may have carried out.

"I suppose I do" he confesses "I was a believer earlier on in my old life, but the behaviour of all the other believers made me lose faith."

"All of them?" probes Gela.

"Yes all of them" he says with conviction and without hesitation.

"Everyone around me, back then I mean, would speak about being devout from one side of their face, then go out and contradict themselves with words from the other side, and their actions."

This causes the nurse to look to him with polite scepticism.

What Jack said was true to his experience and that experience was all he had to go on, but now, as an active member of a community thousands of years later, where he is no longer the secluded teenager living in an urban jungle, he begins to wonder if his knowledge was really broad enough to go by, especially given how isolated he had been.

'And I thought this question was going to make Gela feel uncomfortable!' he thinks to himself, appreciating the ironically.

Gela decides to break the silence with words of her experience.

"You know there were many true believers back then Jack? I learned this for a fact after one of my first Fall experiences."

"Fall experience?"

"I'll explain later, my point is; you were not as alone as you may have thought you were. Even those one-day-per-week lip-service types, often went on to practice what they preached."

Simply being shown that he holds a negative view by someone he trusts, is enough to get Jack to re-examine his views with a fresh perspective.

Based on his relationships now, he realises that he has become less entrenched against many things, which includes religion. He does not want become a believer by any means, but he suddenly finds himself less polarised from the subject.

Gela notices the possible paradigm shift in his way of thinking, so decides that he may now be ready hear what she has to say.

To answer the question on religion within their community, Gela explains.

"Religious beliefs are a personal matter to most people these days, out of choice more than anything. There are still churches, and religious people now have a safe society where they can come together and pray whenever or wherever they wish to, with the focus now being on their own spirituality. Without oppression or any of the other issues they had back in your time, there is no need to "convert the heathens" as some used to say. If you want to share beliefs, go ahead, you will be welcomed by those who share them, and if you don't, you will still have good friends who do."

Even religion, which Jack had been so entrenched against, now seems better in this new world.

He vaguely recalls hearing in his old time that the word "God" had meant "I am". In a way the philosophy of this world had actualised this with humanity's new lease on life. True belief in self and others.

Gela answering his question so matter-of-factly, whilst causing him to question his own views, does make Jack wonder if the nurse held any religious beliefs herself. She then adds.

"You may also be interested to know that a great religious icon was

77

reincarnated around two hundred years ago."

A look of awe comes over Gela as she reminisces about the prophet.

"That person was everything the people of their time had made them out to be, and more. So much more. They were the perfect human, a superhuman, with supernatural abilities. The most kind and loving person anyone had ever met. But she was terribly embarrassed by all of the atrocities that were carried in her former name while she was away."

Upon hearing this dogmatic bombshell, Jack still could not tell whether Gela was religious or not, though she certainly was not "lukewarm" in giving him lots to think about.

Time Goes By

Part III

Present in the dojo today are Jack, Wey, Thyn and Oclea, all poised and awaiting their Sensei's instruction.

Yendo looks over the line of students who stand before him, each face an eager one, their keen expressions serving to inspire his motivation for the morning's class.

"Today we will use our spirit point to lift us into the air" he announces.

Jack looks up to the Hub's grand high ceilings, now realising that they must be so high for more reasons than just acoustics and breathing space alone.

Excitement fills the room as the four pupils mentally prepare themselves.

Their sensei explains the steps involved and what is expected, and as soon as he gives the go ahead, Thyn and Oclea are off in a flash.

He is impressed with Thyn's formidable ability, and even more so with Oclea's control in the air.

"I see you two have been practicing" their sensei complements with a knowing smile.

With the two frequent flyers honing their skills, Yendo uses the opportunity to focus on teaching the newcomers how to fly independently.

Yendo knew of Jack and Wey's brief levitation at the Crag on their second day, he found it a very remarkable feat. Now their teacher aims to have them both able to stream whenever and wherever they wish, should they ever wish to.

"Focus on your centre and listen…" Yendo instructs in his reliably calm voice. While Jack focuses, the high-pitched whine he had heard at the Crag that night returns. The sound echoes throughout his head and he begins to feel light, as if being magnetically drawn up from the floor by an invisible string.

Suddenly, both Jack and Wey gently lift off the floor and into the air, just as they had briefly on their second night.

Levitating comes a lot more naturally to Wey this time, as he steadily breathes in to keep his from composed as he rises.

Jack on the other hand struggles. He finds the lack of gravity to be very off balancing, so much so that he winds up levitating with his feet pointed to the ceiling and his head to the floor. His flailing limbs fail do him any favours whilst upside down.

Yendo helps Jack safely back to the tiled floor, then calmly tells him to start again.

'I did this a few weeks ago, why can't I do it now?' the newcomer thinks in frustration.

Just then, as if reading Jack's thoughts, Yendo calls over to him.

"Don't try to recreate what you did that night at the Crag."

Jack gives the sensei a look of surprise *'Can he read my thoughts?'*

The sensei continues.

"We all do something well, and then we try too hard to recreate it. Don't! Be proud of your achievements, but don't try to relive yesterday, for it might not work today."

Yendo then stops to add.

"And no Jack, I can't read your thoughts, your face gives it all away."

The calm teacher allows an amused grin to escape after watching the newcomer's reaction to his words.

After laughing off his own gullibility on mind-reading, Jack takes in what his sensei had said and releases his tension.

Now instead of striving to levitate, he simply does his best while remaining relaxed.

'What else is there to do? "será será".'

Jack lifts up again, and this time he is better at controlling his position. He lets his body become as light as the sound he hears.

"That's it!" encourages Yendo "Gravity can no longer hold onto you when you let go of all that tension. Well done!"

Jack thought that he would be able to see the slipstreams that he was told of. Surely they would be there in some form through the air when he was ready to fly, but all there is for him in this moment is a feeling, one that tells him to go.

He leaps toward where the notion had taken him and before he knows it, Jack travels the stream which cuts through the air.

Streaming through the air like everyone else in the class proves to be lots of fun, like being on a waterslide, only the chute is invisible and never fixed to the same point. It is an interesting sensation and Jack surmises that *'You must be soft, but also alive, in order to stream'*, a statement which would only make sense to someone who has already experienced the rapids above. With energy coursing through his being, Jack tranquilly traverses one end of the spacious hall to another, at near instant speeds.

It does not feel like he is flying, more like the room is shifting around him. He simply chooses where he wants to go and before he knows it, finds himself there.

After the newcomers both prove themselves to have mastered the basics, Yendo decides to take the class outside for a freer stream in the open air.

Streaming far and wide through the fresh outdoor air is very liberating, especially for both newcomers, whose adrenaline filled screams only go unnoticed thanks to the vast distances between themselves and everyone else.

While wiping away the tears which had been cut into existence by the raw winds ripping past his eyes due to the turbulent speeds, Jack finds himself soaring above and even overtaking birds in the sky.

Passing over an elegant flock blissfully migrating and looking down upon their formation from above, gives Jack a wondrous new perspective of the world which he had never considered. Something so simple, yet so much more, truly a memory to hold on to. To see the birds in flight from above and be able to touch them in mid-flight if you wanted to, makes him wonder what else may now be possible.

Another formative experience from Jack's maiden flight, which proves to be less positive than the birds, is that despite being able to travel great distances in the blink of an eye, through the energy that invisibly courses throughout the air, he finds himself failing to keep up with the rest of the class.

He does manage break-neck speeds, even some fancy manoeuvres, but seeing everyone else racing ahead of him and performing much more sophisticated movements is a little disheartening.

The class soon returns to the ground and the sensei calls an end to practice for today.

Following the end of class, Yendo approaches Jack.

"You were excellent up there kid. Most people can't do what you did, and for a newcomer to do that, well it's really something!"

"Thank you, Sensei" he replies, realising that even though he could not keep up with Wey, Thyn or Oclea, what he did manage to do up there was still way above the norm.

Jack becomes more grateful for his ability to stream, and from his sensei's encouraging words, learns to appreciate this better.

Time Goes By

Part IV

Jack trims back a few leaves, adds some water, then steps back to admire the fruits of his labour.

The surta seed which he had chosen only weeks ago, now blossoms fully as a thriving plant. He decided to name it "Miso" for no reason other than simply taking a liking the name and believing that the name suited his growing friend.

Seeing the plump orange bulbs beginning flourish amongst the leathery dark leaves of the surta plant brings a warm smile to his face.

He goes straight from the dojo and out into the fields to meet up with Thyn, Gela and Wey. Their mission today; to harvest a large section of usuraum plants which were ready for the kitchen.

The four happily work away talking as they picked the food until Jack, Thyn and Gela, all pause to look over at Wey. The newcomer frantically works himself harder and faster than the three of them combined.

"On a mission!!" shouts Jack in a jovial tone.

"Yeah, looks like I've got competition!" agrees Thyn, with his ever-friendly smile.

Despite the humble admiration from his friends, Wey continues to toil, fanatically working up a sweat as if oblivious to everything but the task before him.

Wey enjoyed a challenge too much. He had always made a point of being stronger and faster than he was last time, never competing with anyone but himself. A philosophy which is shared by most people in the world now, but to see someone overworking themselves' in a populated world where there is no shortage of anything is truly a bizarre spectacle.

The four finish their harvest in record time thanks to good teamwork along with Wey's zealous tenacity.

'Whoever said that "many hands make light work" had clearly never met Wey' thinks Jack, realising how many hours his one-man army counterpart had taken off their time.

The group head back to the Hub, satisfied and talking away as they trolley the day's bounty back in carts.

When they near the edge of the fields, Jack notices a man in the distance waving to them as he hurries over.

"Who's this?" he asks, having not seen the man before.

"I don't know" replies Gela.

"I think I've seen him around" adds Thyn.

When the running man reaches them, Jack notices that he bears a slight resemblance to Mr Davis, his next-door neighbour from his past life. Davis had always been in such a foul mood back then, it was nice to see that this visitor with the same face was not angry, though something was clearly troubling him.

The man stops before them, pausing for breath before he speaks.

"Hi, I'm Irmesh from Greenleaves" he says, panting for air while he talks.

Thyn steps forward to welcome the man from their neighbouring community, always happy to greet a visitor.

"Hi Irmesh, my name's Thyn, I have a few streaming friends from your town. What can we do for you?"

With a heavy burden clouding over his face, Irmesh looks into Thyn's eyes, and replies in a manner which is calm, but also carries a note of the utmost urgency.

"I've been sent here with a message from my town."

Gela steps in.

"What's wrong?" she asks with growing concern. The newcomers also pay serious attention as he explains.

"Our crops have failed this time round, and our harvest has fallen short. I've been sent here to ask if we may humbly impose on you for help, until this crisis is over?"

All boys look to Gela, who was the person with seniority and the best among them to answer the call this big.

The nurse smiles her ever soothing smile at their visitor, then answers.

"We have room for two on this mountain pasture."

The statement pleases Irmesh, and perplexes both Jack and Wey.

Relief washes over the visitor who thanks Gela wholeheartedly, before rushing off to give his townspeople the news.

86

As soon as the messenger is gone, and as soon as they realise that this crisis has not flustered Thyn or Gela in the slightest, Jack and Wey begin once again with their newcomer questions, this time with Jack taking the first turn.

"Why was he worried that we might not help him?" he asks, troubled at what the answer could be.

'Is there a sinister side to this world that they have hid from me?'

Gela notices his concern and explains.

"Humans will always help those in need Jack, our town prides itself on this truth. But Irmesh was wise not to take our help for granted, he only saw the edge of our fields. For all he knew we could have been having the same problems as his town, and it's only manners to ask."

"Fair enough" Jack nods approvingly.

Wey then steps in next with the next question.

"What's this mountain pass you spoke of?"

"That's *"mountain pasture"* Wey" corrects Gela, "It's a saying in these parts which means "we can accommodate you"."

"Yeah man its colloquial" adds Thyn, before turning to Jack.

"You might wanna run ahead and tell Yendo we're gonna have some guests tonight..."

Dinner tonight at the Hub, and the many other dining venues throughout Larutan, proves to be an extravagant event for all.

More tables had been brought into the Hall and almost every seat was taken. The room still remained grand and spacious as ever in spite of the influx.

With the notable reduction in space came a vast increase in people sharing good times.

Yendo, with the help of Jack and many others, had managed to prepare enough food for all of the regulars and guest diners in a timely fashion.

Being worn out from all the running around he had done preparing in the kitchen, Jack now sits at his table too tired to fully appreciate the food. Though being tired did not get in the way of enjoying the company of his friends and neighbours.

While he talks away, Jasper happily goes round the diners in the Hall, moving from table to table to loftily bask in the affection of her admirers after drawing in their attention with a look from her bright round eyes.

Gela talks away to Irmesh who sits next to her, while across from them, Wey catches up with the tortie-twins. Thyn, who had chosen to dine at the Hall tonight, is joined at the table by his high-flying visitor friend, the one he raced with on the newcomers' first night at the Crag.

Next to Jack is a girl from his own town called Emba, a scientist who is a few years younger than he, and seemingly a lot smarter.

There is something very familiar about Emba, though he could not place it, but instead of finding out why she seemed so familiar to him, Jack decides to focus on asking her about the science of this world.

Jack had not liked scientists, nor the other so called "professionals" in his old time. They used to always take the easy route, with no trace of compassion, as they ticked boxes to receive their pay without any thought or concern. However, he was sure that the scientists now, along with everything else, would be better.

He does his usual routine of asking many newcomer questions, and Emba on her part kindly answers them all in polite detail.

"So you're telling me that science is now holistic?"

"That's correct Jack. We have found and continue to find cures using the scientific method and the ingredients that nature has given us. Those poisonous chemicals and their side effects you've told me of would never be accepted now."

"And there's no testing on animals?"

"Indeed Jack, torturing animals is unthinkable."

"Things really have come a long way! I even like scientists now!" he declares.

"Glad to hear it" replies Emba, who gives a friendly laugh with a gentle warm glow.

"Though I don't like the sound of those "box-tickers" you described from your old time. They are the antithesis of who we are today."

On top of appearing familiar to Jack, he also finds Emba to be a very agreeable person with a kind nature.

Throughout the night, the conversation of the Hall flowed and laughter erupted at intervals all round.

Jack enquires into what "science work" his new friend was doing at the moment.

Welcoming the interest, the very intelligent girl happily explains to him that she is currently researching a project which involves a new way of converting the remaining traces of inorganic waste, which had been left in the ground over the ages, into contemporary degradable material.

"Though that research will be put on hold for now, while I help with Greenleaves's food problem" she adds.

Everyone is so selfless now' Jack thinks to himself, feeling so proud to be a just small part of it with his humble efforts in the fields and kitchen.

***

After a week with guests from Greenleaves living in Larutan, the farmers and scientists from both towns finally come up with the solution of building a "farming-metropolis" on the deserted edge of Greenleaves.

Now, instead the barren stone ground which resides just outside of Greenleaves, the town would benefit from a cityscape of giant greenhouses instead of rocks. It would provide the people with a food surplus and prevent another shortage from possibly ever happening again.

Everyone from both towns look forward to the endeavour with the most uplifting positivity, so much so, that not a single person had any doubt of their mission's success.

Weeks later, "Farm City" as it had been dubbed upon completion, flourishes. Irmesh's face was a picture to behold when he laid eyes on the good people's creation. Such elation. His expression was also good for Jack to see, as he always thought that Mr Davis, who Irmesh so closely resembled, deserved to smile. To see Irmesh smiling as happily as he did at the sight of his town's triumph, gave Jack a pleasant closure to the memory of Mr Davis. Farm city now successfully provides for the town of Greenleaves so well, that the townspeople had already begun sending their surplus crops on to the neighbouring towns, especially Larutan, in gratitude for all the help they had given them.

One day shortly after Farm City's completion; Jack, Wey and Gela, along with little Jasper, all travel to Greenleaves carrying a portable sack filled with new seed varieties for neighbours.

As Wey streams back and forth in figure eights high in the air above them, Jack steadily walks along the long road which brims with lush greenery to either side, with Gela walking next to him, and Jasper prowling ahead in the distance.

As Wey loops around overhead, Jack's attention is down, focused on the paving on which he walks.

Instead of bricks, dirt, or tar, these roads which were created from waste that once filled the ocean, now showed cubist artwork.

91

'*It's amazing what they can do with refuse from the sea!*' thinks Jack as he walks further down the road.

"I'm glad someone still appreciates the lost skill of walking" says a smiling Gela, stirring Jack from his thoughts.

He looks up at Wey showing off in the air.

"Yeah, streaming is nice, but I'm grateful that my legs work." he replies, before adding "I'll use them to make my body the best functioning machine it can possibly be."

A pleasantry which catches the Gela's interest.

"That's a great way of looking at it. Gratitude! From now on, I'm going to focus more on being grateful when I walk too."

"You didn't already?" asks the newcomer, raising a questioning eyebrow to playfully feign drama.

"Well it's all a matter of perception Jack. A matter of perspective and interpretation too." answers the nurse

She then indicates the thriving green bushes to either side of them.

"The leaves on this bright summer's day look a vibrant lime green to me, but in your eyes they may appear a bright chartreuse. As I'm looking at them, I'm thinking of my past experiences in the town up ahead, while you may be thinking of what you did before coming here."

"Everyone is different" agrees Jack, but Gela is not yet finished.

"I enjoy a crisp winter, where you Jack have told me that you love nothing better than a bright, hot summer. I also noticed this when we connected.

92

"Knowledge and direction are yours and yours alone. You can still share your experiences, but when you do you create something entirely new in another person. A new truth. I've always focused on my destination when travelling, and some people think about what they are travelling away from, but now after this conversation, I'm going focus more on my gratitude for the journey."

"Wow…" Jack does not know what else to say.

'Gela is sometimes a little reserved, but then out of nowhere, BANG! She will drop a philosophical bombshell on you."

This line of thought gets his mind going again.

'On my first day, Gela said that Gaia, the Earth itself, had brought me back for a reason.'

Jack inwardly starts laughing at himself, as he examines his thoughts from that first day with the benefit of hindsight.

'I thought that I was going to be some kind of superhero. So naive and idealistic… Haha! Listen to me, I'm old before my time!'

Realising that he has come a long way since that first day, he looks round at his situation here and now.

Gela is accompanying him on the most visually pleasing road that he has ever walked upon. His friend Wey looms smoothly above, like a dry leave caught in a breeze. All the while his faithful companion, Jasper, trots on before or behind them, but never with, as the cat is too proud for that. They are all his friends and they all share in the same mission, the same purpose, and that is to make the most of this beautiful sunny day, while making sure their neighbouring friends can enjoy a life as good as theirs.

Jack may not be some rockstar superhero as "Gaia choosing him" had led him to anticipate, but he does have his own special place here in this world, which makes him feel like one.

Cherishing his complete life with good friends and a great place to live, where he can make a difference and contribute, he looks over to see the sunlight glistening over Gela's gentle features.

'Such a beautiful day.'

From reflecting on his situation, Jack comes to the realisation that everything is consent. We consent to who we are. We consent to the society in which we live. We consent to the unavoidable truth of love. We even consent to taking offense, after all; you're giving the other person permission to alter your state of mind. It really is an ideal world, even when it doesn't seem like it.

Looking on ahead to where the artistic road is taking him, an incorrigible smile begins to strengthen his face.

Jack takes in a deep breath as he continues to walk, and then out loud, still wearing the same resilient smile, he decides.

"I choose this."

Time Goes By

Part V

While making his way to the dojo, Jack looks up to find the sky ablaze with the deepest shades of orange that he has ever seen. This celestial procession is a far more emotive sight than the pale off-white apricot that he had become accustomed to.

These deep fiery ambers could not have been any further from his remembered blue sky, that precious sapphire which he yearned for so badly. All the same, to see this burning nebula stretch across the vast reaches of the heavens, was to witness nature's most primal persona baring its most ferocious flair for all to see.

At a glance, this is enough to liberate what lies dormant in a person's soul.

Today in the dojo, Jack finds that there is only himself and Mantha awaiting their sensei on the stone tiles.

He knew that Wey and Thyn were out streaming somewhere, but he could not account for anyone else. Even little Jasper had run off.

Both Jack and Mantha make a standing bow when Yendo arrives, showing respect to their teacher as he enters.

The sensei's presence alone is enough to fill the large, near empty hall, with a contagiously positive strength.

"It would appear that we have a smaller class today" says the teacher with a tranquil smile.

That calm smile eases any tensions the two students may have carried, and with this, they realise that the power a person can gain from relaxing completely is truly a wonder.

Looking at his two students, Yendo decides on today's lesson.

"A powerful sky and low numbers, this is a fine opportunity for us to practice the waves" …

Yendo takes Jack and Mantha out to an empty beach where the tide is constant.

Standing before the waves, their teacher deeply inhales the rich sea air before addressing them.

"The only opponent you will ever have to face in the dojo is yourself. There is also no opponent here, but there is a new challenge that awaits you."

He signals to the tide behind him then turns to face the waves.

Maintaining his posture with a bend in his knees, the teachers centres himself the ground beneath his feet, then extends up onto his toes, reaching out to the furthest limits his hands could reach.

Then he begins.

Yendo lowers himself down to a centred position once more and holds his hands out, as though to gently push away an invisible barrier.

The students notice the back and forward flow of the sea's waves begin to

96

hasten as Yendo sends his energy out.

'Surely it's just coincidence?'

Had it not been for his well-earned faith in his sensei, Jack would have been convinced that what he is witnessing was an elaborate hoax.

'"More powerful than most people from my old time would even allow themselves to imagine!"' he recollects thinking.

Suddenly, with the force from one powerful gesture, Yendo goes from gently quickening the tide, to sending waves forcefully out back and forth. The students stand awed as their teacher shakes the tide at abrupt speeds.

The power-waves continue get thrown as far as the eye can see, until the Sensei decides to send out one gigantic surge, so huge that it makes the water closest to the beach split down the middle, receding the shoreline to expose the bed of wet sand where the sea had once slept.

Jack notices that there are no fish on the vacant seabed.

'Did Yendo know there were no fish here? Or did the fish leave when they sensed him coming?'

The water travels far away until eventually a tall rebound wave returns with a colossal roar.

To Jack, the white foam of this immense tide, vengeful under burning orange, akin to red, in the sky, looks like the gargantuan jaws of an otherworldly lion rushing to devour them.

With no possibility of ever escaping the path of this monster which rampages toward them under the fiery heavens, both pupils nervously

97

accept their fate and silently ask themselves how this could be.

The two reach panic stations as the immense tide draws in so close that they could no longer see the red sky above, their hearts pound frantically as they taste the salty spray from the roaring tide in the air.

Suddenly and gently, Yendo slows the wave down, until the sky-tall surge benignly loses its height, and returns to its natural ebb and flow.

Once the tide had returned to its normal rhythm, Yendo brings his attention back to Jack and Mantha, inviting the two to come forward and test the waves themselves.

The pupils warily yet excitedly step forward. The time to hone the reach of their ki had come.

"Imbibe it all, breathe in, then send your will out before you. The waves will move because you will them to move."

Both Jack and Mantha extend out, settling down into the same low stance their sensei had taken.

"Focus on your breathing and let it all come naturally" instructs their sensei, continuing to coach them with his words of wisdom.

The two struggle to even shake the water.

"Reach out with your mind, have the intention in your hands, and make it all possible with a steady outbreath."

The two focus hard but fruitlessly as they plough ahead with great effort, never giving in.

Their determination builds and builds, meanwhile the strain of their effort becomes more and more, until finally a core teaching of ki dawns on them - relax.

"Breath is reassuringly predictable, yet it is not something you can plan. Simply breathe and forget about what might be."

Both students let go out their doubts. The relaxation restores their natural positivity and confidence.

"Each breath is unique like a wave."

The tide before them starts to become a little choppy.

"Breathe in for energy, and out for serenity."

Jack stands before the water, looking out at the waves coming in from as far out as his eyes would allow.

He believes he can see currents of his own energy travelling out from his fingertips, out towards the water to stir the tide under the angry red sky.

The idea that the transparent gales of colour which he sees slowly projecting from his hands are not real does occur to Jack, however, the visualisation of his intention makes the manifestation of his energy as real to him as the waves themselves.

With the desire to make the water move in his mind, he relaxes more and begins to send out more ki to sway the waves further.

An impressed Yendo smiles at his progress and continues to guide them.

"Your breath is your best friend; it has always been there throughout your entire life. Just as the waves have been there throughout the life of the Earth."

Finally, after completely letting go of any and all negativity, the waves begin to sway beyond choppy as Jack finds the confidence to send them further out to sea.

At witnessing the newcomer's success, a sunny smile beams from Mantha's round face.

She too finds that breathing in tranquilly while sending out her own energy, allows her to throw the waves as far back as her mind would reach.

"That's it!" encourages Yendo "Realise that in this world your body is only the tip of the iceberg".

The energy from Jack and Mantha goes on to push the waves out even further.

"Your essence will reach out as far as you will imagine".

The waves now take longer to return as their positive energies go out even further.

"Allow your ki to fill up your entire world here and now."

They watch the waves travel out far beyond what their eyes could physically perceive, then slowly return at their will. Both pupils realise that this exercise and the theory behind it, is about using the world to control yourself. A perplexing concept which cannot be grasped logically. The waves could only be understood at another level, a level which they had both found today at the beach.

Jack and Mantha attained something special today.

Standing upon the sandy shore with a joyous air of familiarity in themselves and in the world around them, both students look to each other in sweet camaraderie, then to their teacher in gratitude.

"Well done you two!" congratulates Yendo. "I now invite you to describe your experiences of mastering the waves."

Without words, the two look to each other and decide that Jack should go first.

He steps forward to share his perspective, holding out his hand to indicate the environment around him.

"Today we stood under a ferocious sky that was beautiful at the same time. At first nature controlled us with fear, then we controlled nature with kindness. I now realise that this, all of this, all that exists; is mine. Not "mine" like a possession, but "mine" as in; me and my surroundings are one and cannot exist in any other way."

Summarising his experiences into words had always been tricky for Jack, now to try summarising an experience as abstract as this one, proves to be near impossible, still he continues.

"I don't know if I complete the world, or if it's the world that completes me..."

Yendo notices his discomfort and comes to the rescue.

"Very good Jack! I understand exactly what you're saying, and I often find myself reaching a similar conclusion".

Being understood makes Jack feel like a weight had been lifted from his shoulders, which is ideal when talking about the indefinite constructs from your inner self.

A smile of relief is his reply to the sensei.

Yendo nods encouragingly, then turns his attention to Mantha.

Being a very eloquent young lady, Mantha is more than ready to vocalise her experiences from today.

"To me, the waves have been a microcosm of our relationship with the world.

"The world that each of us lives in is small when compared to the Earth we walk on. There may be oceans across this vast physical existence that we share, but when you jump in a puddle it is the rest of us who get splashed. When you throw a stone into the water, the ripple you create will reach out to touch us all. The effect we all have on our loved ones is life changing, and the life changing impressions we can make on an acquaintance, even a stranger, is lasting."

A silent moment of reflection follows Mantha's summary.

Jack is impressed by how well she put it. The meaning of her words resonate with him powerfully after today's lesson.

Yendo too, nods his approval.

""Impressions"! Very good Mantha, well done! You two have both achieved excellence today, you should be proud. Now let's be getting back to our commitments at the Hub."

As Yendo goes to lead them back, his step is halted by a question from Jack.

"Wait Sensei! Can I ask how you would describe your experience of the waves?"

Yendo smiles and in a light tone answers.

"Of course you can Jack. My summary is much like yours and Mantha's.

"When making the waves, I often find that although this world completes me, I can still make my own lasting impression on the world. It is a bit like numbers in a way. One person may reach nine by adding six and three, while another may find it by adding four and five. All roads lead to the same destination when the waves are concerned, and our ki is a lot like the waves; unique and never-ending. The more ki you give, means the more ki you will have. We never deplete ourselves by using it."

Time Goes By

Part VI

A gentle breeze carries the word of a sweet song past Gela's ear in the fields.

"Tomorrow..." is all she manages to hear of the song, and though it is only one word, the lyric captures her interest so much that she decides to follow where it had come from.

Making her way through the sunny fields, she begins to catch more of the melody while trailing its musical current in the air.

"...all true..."

"...being here..."

"...anything..."

Hearing more song fragments perks her curiosities further, as she continues to follow in wonder.

The words become clearer as she draws closer, passing over the sunlit mound which separates her from the singer, and at last she finds the source from where the song had come.

On the other side of the mound is Jack, reaping grain whilst singing a song of hope from his past life.

"It's alright,

It's okay,

The future is here, there'll be a way!"

Gela had no idea that his interest in music was so strong that he could carry a tune from thousands of years ago.

Noticing that the song had ended, she applauds the working boy and calls over to him.

"Well the future is certainly here for you".

A startled Jack looks over to find Gela giving him an ovation. His ears go red from being caught singing when he had not even realised he was doing it.

In an attempt to hide his bashfulness, he quickly replies.

"I guess that's why the song came to mind."

Gela with great interest in both her newcomer and his music, decides to ask more about what he was singing.

"Where many songs from your old time about the future?"

"Only some. Most songs would come and go, and most of them didn't really mean anything. But sometimes, just sometimes, a song really would change the world."

"That's very interesting" replies Gela, eager to learn more "Where songs about the future a favourite of yours?"

Jack ponders his tastes in music for a few seconds.

"No, not really. My favourites were usually instrumentals. Though I did enjoy songs with deep, meaningful lyrics... abstract ones about life."

Taking a moment to consider his music, Gela smiles her reassuring smile to Jack, who continues to blush from being caught singing unawares.

105

After this quick momentary smile in silence, Gela decides to let him in on one of her activities outside of the Hub.

"I'm meeting up with some friends later in town today, and we're going to be making music. Would you like to come?"

Having never made music before, ever, or even been invited to anything like this either, Jack gladly accepts this kind invitation, feeling very cherished and included by the offer.

After doing their bit for Larutan in the fields, Jasper re-joins Jack, and along with Gela, the three make their way into town, heading to an old building known only as "The Space".

Every building which Jack had seen in this new world so far had looked so fresh and modern like the Hub. The Space however proves to be very different.

Outside he can tell that the building is old just from looking at it. Old but still fit for purpose.

The other structures around Larutan look much more sophisticated and futuristic than the Space, but to Jack this less impressive building, found on the corner of the town's oldest quarter, with age setting in all around, possesses a charm which could never be manufactured.

At first sight, before they even step through the front door, he believes he can feel a pulse emanating from the old building. An energetic vibrance calling to those who were ready to listen.

The pulse emanates louder and louder as they draw closer, then once inside, mingling through the creative types who frequent the establishment, Jack could definitely feel the pulse as though it were beating through his own heart.

Noticing the awestricken newcomer taking in his surroundings, Gela decides to tell him a little of the building's history.

"This place has been around for a hundred years, Jack. It has been home to many artists, some of the finest that Larutan has ever seen."

Her expression fills with pride, and the nurse becomes starry-eyed while looking round at all the history displayed on the walls.

"Originally the Space was a studio for the great artist Gasterry, and over the years it has become a home away from home to artists of every kind. This place has seen the best plays and concerts that have ever been performed in Larutan…"

Gela becomes aware that she may rambling a little, so decides to finish off with a joyous "And now we're standing in it!"

"I'm honoured to be here" replies Jack, attempting to shield his awe with playful sarcasm.

To get to the jam session, they proceed past the sculptors and the man playing the piano on the ground floor. Move on up to the second floor, where they pass a friendly mime in the corridor, to finally enter a sizeable room which looks out onto the town square.

What Jack finds in this room is a wondrous contrast from the old world he

107

used to know.

He finds an inviting setting stocked with a variety of musical instruments and packed with the most exotic people he has ever encountered.

"Gela!" is the roar from all present as his party enters.

"Hi everyone!" she calls back, giving them all a wave before indicating to her guests. "I'd like you to meet Jack and his friend Jasper. Jack's going to jam with us today."

Jack is welcomed warmly by the group and is introduced to a few of the musicians, along with their instruments, while the rest get ready.

The first musician to introduce themselves personally to Jack is Upblar, a large friendly man wearing an outfit that looks a lot like a dress to the newcomer.

Upblar gives him the first handshake that he has been given since being reincarnated, and after the handshake, shows Jack his musical instrument of a flute looking pipe-organ, referred to as an "imbre".

Upblar tells Jack that he is traditionally old fashioned, hence the handshake and the choice of a more rustic instrument.

'Such a friendly man' Jack thinks to himself.

He is also warmly welcomed by Vanamada, or "Vana for quickness". She is a tall slender woman, dressed in tight silver clothing whilst wearing her instrument of a thin metal glove called a "shred".

Vana demonstrates the shred by simply plucking sound from the air using her gloved fingers. It creates high pitched whines and deep low drones, just like the electric guitars from Jack's old time. With keen interest he begins emulating her movements.

'Such a cool instrument!'

Noticing the newcomer copying her moves, Vana asks him if he practices GaiKiZen.

Once she learns that he does, Vana tells him that she used to train under Yendo when she was younger. She also tells him that the shred can only be played by a musician who can harness their ki.

'Ki music! My kinda thing!'

The last person to introduce themselves personally to Jack, is Gwarysta, a jovial woman who is possibly even more welcoming than Upblar.

She shows Jack the "theleon"; a round vase looking instrument which is said to play music from the soul.

She demonstrates the theleon by blowing into the opening at the top of a clay pot, then from inside comes a light of cheery bright orange with the radiance of a lit golden lamp.

Jack immediately identifies this glow as the colour of Gwarysta's aura.

Along with the glowing colour comes a weird and wonderful sound from the pot, a soothing sound, much like the unbroken echo of a sweet woman's voice.

"This is the sound of my heart centre, the unstruck cord that lies within me."

Gwarysta then moves her hands though the bright orange air around the vase, shaping the sweet-sounding light into whatever tone she desired.

109

'*That's amazing!*' the newcomer thinks to himself, as he watches the mix of music and colour warp through the air.

With most of the musicians ready, Jack is encouraged to pick up one of the many unused instruments that lie in the room to join in when the jam it starts.

He timidly warns everyone that he has never played any instrument before, but the group pleasantly assure him that he has nothing to fear.

He scans the room and finds an idle shred glove lying on top of an unused drum-set. Quickly, he chooses this to be his instrument and though it was a rushed decision, he is happy with the choice.

Noticing how pleased Jack looks with the shred, Gela comments.

"I thought you would have chosen the theleon."

He smiles to the nurse as if to say '*You know me too well*' before verbally answering.

"It was between this and the theleon, but the theleon seems a little above my pay grade at the moment."

A friendly laugh escapes Gela, who is possibly the only person in the room who would understand the term "pay grade" from her work with newcomers.

Jack then enthusiastically adds.

"Plus, this is my chance to play an actual air-guitar! And I get to use my ki!!"

After comically nodding in satisfaction over his own choice, Jack looks to Gela, and notices a lack of instrument in her hands.

He asks the nurse what she intends to play, and at this, Gela picks up a large ukulele.

Looking to the instrument with a fondness in her eyes, while tuning its strings with tender care, Gela tells him.

"This is my musical friend. We met in here about three years ago and have been inseparable ever since."

The wooden instrument clearly held a special place in the nurse's heart.

"It's time!" Gwarysta announces, bringing silence and anticipation to the room.

Little Jasper runs beneath a table, bracing herself for the loud impact of sudden noise, but the next thing to be heard is a broad introductory hum from several instruments throughout the room. The humming includes the sound of theleons which light up the studio with their kind philharmonic colour.

The hum is audible, but not by no means overwhelming, and it is smoothly joined by the sharper instruments, such as the shreds.

The riffs and beats meld together to create a harmony which flows into a soft enigmatic melody. A harmony so soothing that little Jasper comes out from hiding under the table, to sit atop and enjoy the sound which has connected everyone in the room.

Jack, who is unsure of what to do with his shred, looks round to the other musicians and begins to wonder just how he is supposed to play. Gela notices this and quietly whispers to him.

"There's no wrong way, just play how you feel."

At this he raises his metal-gloved hand and recreates the movements which Vana had shown him, but to his disappointment the shred emits no sound.

He quickly remembers that the shred must be played using ki. So taking in a clean breath, he lets his entire body become light while allowing gravity to intensify its pull, then this time with feeling, strikes the air.

With life in his movement and energy in his thoughts, the whine of an electric guitar travels from where his hand had stricken, joining in the melody of the room.

'Not bad for a guy who has never made music before' he thinks, pleased with his creation.

While continuing to add to the music, a mint green mist with hews of emerald begin to gather round his hands. The mist lightly fills the space in which his shred create music, and from watching it, he immediately knows what he is seeing.

'This is my aura!'

After the self-discovery of what his own aura looks like, Jack becomes aware that he had never felt so relaxed anywhere as he did making music here.

Feeling serene and looking round at the harmony which flows across the room, Jack discovers a new nirvana. It is as if all the interesting people here had let their souls run free to dance through the air, their physical forms remaining behind to smoothly make sweet music in the tangible world below.

When the music was over, everyone in the room simply sits back and relaxes.

Friendship and kudos are shared by all, then one by one the musicians call it a day and begin to head off.

Gwarysta however, made a point of thanking Jack for coming along, congratulating him on successfully contributing to the melody of his first ever jam.

The two get talking about the various instruments and harmonies for much longer than she had intended to, though she was still happy to talk away all the same.

Their conversation grows deeper and deeper, about music and about life. They talk away until Gwarysta eventually tells Jack a little something to finish off the evening, a little something which reminds him of Yendo's teachings.

"Life is vibration and that energy is in everything.

"I think the best use of this energy is when we create our wonderful music. It exists in all things: What we see with our eyes is the vibration of light, and what we can hear is the vibration of sound. If you are ever unwell, the best remedy is movement. Energy is what we use to move, it's our life force after all. We are born, our heart beat for the first time, and that single heartbeat echoes for a lifetime."

Not knowing what else to say, Jack thanks his maestro sincerely with all his gratitude, not only for generously sharing her music with him, but also for giving him a teaching that would stay with him forever.

The newcomer's gratefulness gives Gwarysta an even bigger smile if that were possible.

"Thanks again for coming Jack, it's been great having you here."

Time Goes By

Part VII

"Are you ready Jack?"

Whilst wearing a solemn expression upon his usually bright face, and carrying with it, an uncharacteristically serious tone, Thyn asks.

Although the day is sunny and warm, the waterfall in which they stand at resides within a cool shadow of its own creation.

Looking over to the clear stream as it gently crashes down into the shallow pool below, makes Jack second guess whether he really wants to do this. Perhaps his thirst for new experiences had finally gone too far? Then again, how can anyone be free if they let their fear control them?

After a short thoughtful spell in the lovely aroma of the dark fall's moisture, mixed with the scents of the surrounding sun kissed forest, he looks to Thyn and replies.

"Yes"

Only moments ago, Wey had emerged from the Waterfall of Knowledge which Thyn had shown them today.

Wey appears very relaxed after his experience, as if he had found some kind of consolation in the answers that were given to him.

Feeling that Wey had now been given long enough to regain his bearings, Jack decides to appease his own curiosity and ask his fellow newcomer exactly what he learned.

Taking in smooth long breaths, Wey slowly turns his head to face him, then once eye contact is made, his fellow newcomer simply replies in a manner as calm as can be.

"Oh, nothing and everything. You'll know when you go in."

'Who would have thought that knowledge could make someone so mellow?' Jack thinks, as he steps forward for his turn.

Removing his footwear, Jack rolls up his trousers and steps into the stream.

The tepid currents caress his feet and ankles as he wades toward the Fall, tentatively splashing and sploshing with each step.

Thyn and Wey look on, both hopeful that Jack will discover the knowledge he seeks.

Earlier Thyn had told them that a Fall experience can change a person. He even said that when someone immerses themselves in the water, it is Gaia, the Earth itself, who decides what they need to know.

Jack does have a few questions in the back of his mind when going in, but he wisely chooses to enter without any expectation, confident that he will be given all he needs to know by the Earth.

Thyn also told the newcomers that he has yet to meet someone who emerged from the waterfall unsatisfied. Even if the only thing the person learned was that they already have all the knowledge they needed, to have the Earth itself tell you this is enough to change everything.

Jack bravely hides any second thoughts he may have been carrying, as he slowly takes his last few steps and immerses himself within the cascade.

At first he feels the overwhelming chill of the water as it rushes his senses with a brisk freeze, then suddenly someone turns out the lights.

In the blink of an eye the outside world had vanished, and Jack finds himself left in alone in the darkness with only his own thoughts for company.

The darkness feels like forever extended to the lonesome boy.

He waits and he waits, and the days go by as he continues to wait. Monotonous, tedious days, all made worse by his loneliness.

He finds himself no longer waiting for knowledge, but for a friend to end his isolation. He waits, in the hope of finding an exit in the never-ending darkness.

The days continue to roll by, days without light, without sound, without even so much as touch. So many days in this dark place outside of the real world. Where had the forest gone? Where are his friends now?

Negative thoughts from his past life begin to return, haunting him as if he were reliving those horrific days now.

'What is the point in anything when everything means nothing?

…Half the people out there are overworked to death. The other half are kept from contributing and starve. And you can bet your last penny that it's the best people out there who are the first to go…

…In the worthless society, the worthwhile are done for…

…I've spent my whole life waiting to live… waiting to die…

…If you sleep outside in nature then you're sleeping under the stars… if you sleep outside in society, on that grimy cold cement, then you're sleeping

117

rough. The difference made by all the noise, pollution, fabricated light, filth, slime, grime, and crime… A huge difference…

…If the world is indeed round and surrounded by a galaxy; does that make it a celestial asylum for the criminally insane?

…All I wanted was to live.'

These thoughts continue to course through his mind, making him grow colder, as if he were standing in that pale unforgiving society now, the place where the cruel freeze was magnified by its echo which spread throughout the cityscape of cement.

That is until he finally shakes those thoughts and steps out from his own "shadows" to remain mindful.

This isolation would have destroyed most people, but Jack stays strong, never letting his sanity waver. He learned to discard such negative thoughts when living a miserable lonesome life in his old time, a practice which had come in handy now.

His thoughts had become a reliable companion back in his old life, and they remain reliable now in the abyss.

Though he doesn't let the isolation get to him, Jack does have growing concerns when he realises that he has been stuck here for days now, worse still; he has not yet eaten or even felt hunger. This would not end well.

He suddenly hears a sound in the distance, but from which direction?

He looks around in the darkness, only to find more darkness.

'Did I imagine it?'

He hears a noise again.

'The same noise?'

This time in the distance behind him.

He quickly turns around to find where it had come from before it could vanish again, only to be immediately blown away by an onslaught of sound and vision.

The intensity of it all hits him with the might of a sledgehammer as it rockets past like a whirlwind.

'Is this experience really so loud? Or have I spent too much time in the emptiness?'

Amidst the colour and sound, Jack begins to see moments in history that took place after his first life. The word "see" being used lightly, as in actual fact he bears witness to nothing with his eyes, but with his mind. As if the images of blinding intensity were projecting straight into his consciousness with the sound to match.

The history he sees is exactly how he predicted the future would be before he departed.

Things kept getting worse throughout the years. Oppression would take over absolutely, then revolution would fend it off, bringing about a false resolution, which once again became oppression.

Civilisation waltzed back and forth through the terror of the few and the terror of the many, neither of which particularly distinguishable when evil people were at the helm. But even in the darkest of days, there would still

119

be people, good people, there to do what they could even when they were outnumbered and out of favour.

Ultimately after ages of chaos, revolution was finally brought about in the way that was always meant to be, resulting in the "happily ever after" that Jack now knows in Larutan.

He sees that the world now, after ages of healing and harmony, is truly the best time to be alive. Not that this was news to him.

In a way being able to live here and now, and achieve your dreams, is the Earth's way of rewarding humanity for finally finding peace.

'Is that why it brings people back? So they can live out the life that they were always supposed to?'

Jack's eyes spring open as he deeply inhales.

He staggers out from underneath the shadowy waterfall and back into the light.

It is daytime outside and the fresh rush of oxygen makes the colour of his surroundings appear more exuberant in his vision.

In the beautifully bright blinding sun he notices Thyn and Wey standing on a nearby ledge, and calls over to them, asking how long it had been since he entered the waterfall.

"Only a few minutes" Thyn calls back.

Jack simply stands there lost for words. All that exploration, all that torment, the final resolution. How could it only have been a few minutes?

"So how did you find it?" Wey calls over with a knowing grin.

After adjusting to their new levels of consciousness and sharing what they had learned from their Fall experiences, it was soon time for the boys to get back to their day jobs in town.

"Have fun in the fields" Jack calls to his friends as they part company.

After Jack thanks Thyn once again for giving him and Wey yet another memorable experience, his two friends head to the fields making Jack's journey to the Hub a solitary one.

Earlier today his faithful Jasper had run off at the mention of water, which made the trek back to the Hub now, a prime opportunity to reflect on what was learned.

The knowledge he gained simply served to reaffirm what he already knew, or at least what he thought he had known. However, having the Earth itself confirm your understanding changes everything. Jack now feels as though he understands the world at an emotional level, and not just a technical one.

This communion with Gaia had given him a new confidence.

Feeling very secure and very complete, he proudly marches on through the forest stoutly with his chin raised high, all the while exploring what is new in his mind.

'Life is beautiful really when I think about it. There were lots of good people around when I was young. I just let the bad element get to me and crowd them out. I'm grateful to have crossed paths with them all, the good and the

bad. Particularly the good, obviously, who I wish I'd known better.'

Along the way he comes across some strange crimson berries growing from a shrub at the side of the path.

Like everything else in this new world, these bright red berries with patches of midnight blue look as though they are fresh and bursting with juice.

He decides to pluck one for a taste, anticipating a sweet mixture of cranberry and blueberry, however those expectations are soon dashed when he finds the berry has no flavour besides some bitterness.

He quickly swallows the disappointing fruit and goes to set off again, only to find his legs won't work.

His feet suddenly become as lead weights and it is a struggle to move.

The struggle to lift his legs alone leaves him short of breath, then fatigue strikes from nowhere, causing him to stagger about like a drunk trying to regain their balance.

Barely able to open his eyelids, much less focus on anything with his eyes, Jack becomes more and more light-headed as the pupils of his eyes begin to dart about uncontrollably.

'This can't be the "elevator" again?' he asks himself, remembering his last moments on the hospital bed in the past.

Overwhelmed by the invisible pull which drags him down, Jack falls, out cold before his body hits the ground.

***

Jack opens his eyes to find himself lying on a comfortable bed in a gently lit room.

The first thing he notices is the strange, yet soothing aroma of summer flowers which fills the sizeable space, and a subtle, more pungent note of raw onion hiding discretely in the background.

"Welcome back" says the voice of an elegant lady in a pristine tone.

Attempting to rise to see who is addressing him, Jack finds that he has no energy to pull himself up, or even turn his head.

The speaker places a gentle hand on his shoulder to encourage him not to move.

He looks up to see to whom the hand belongs and finds a petite lady with short platinum hair standing over him, smiling down with a gentle kindness.

"It's okay" she says in a voice as soft as a note from a harp.

"My name's Aniesth and I'm here to help."

It turns out that the berry which Jack had eaten on his way back from the Fall, had been a poison "rumery" berry, a deadly nerve toxin which had come very close to finishing him.

Luckily his faithful companion Jasper, had gone out looking for her person when his visit to the Fall had overran.

Jasper managed to catch sight of Jack just as he fell and immediately went for help.

Now Jack found himself in the care of the Hub's specialist healer, Aneisth, who had been tasked with restoring the newcomer back to perfect health.

"So you ate a rumery berry… bad move" she says in an attempt to start some light conversation.

"I wouldn't have eaten one, if someone had bothered to warn me about them" complains Jack in response.

Noticing his bitter-side returning, he decides to be a little more thoughtful and good humoured, first impressions are very important after all.

"…and to think I had just left the Waterfall of Knowledge. Goes to show that absolute knowledge doesn't give you all the answers. Pun definitely intended."

"I see I have a comic philosopher on my hands" the nurse replies, in summary of his two answers.

Unfortunately Jack's humorous side is short lived, as it fades when he ponders his karma.

"No. The only thing funny about me is the farce of something like this happening anytime I begin to feel complete."

Aneisth takes a quick moment to study her patient who lies motionless on the bed.

He seems content to her, like someone who had finally found peace after a very long search. His green aura even shows him to be a playful individual with great curiosity. Yet his words do not reflect this.

'I think he is holding on to the scars from his distant past.'

124

With a deep breath, Aneisth decides that the time to heal these scars had come.

"Do you see that crystal above you on the ceiling?" she asks, pointing upward.

Jack does his best to nod.

"I want you to focus all of your attention on that crystal and think of the colour yellow."

He gazes up to the sizable rock above as the nurse brings her hands to either side of his head.

Though she does not physically touch him, Jack is certain that he can feel an energy radiating from her hands, some kind of magnetic heat travelling to the centre of his head.

'What is she doing?'

The nurse detects his curiosities and concern within the invisible sphere of her hands and instructs him to relax.

Becoming aware of his tension, Jack realises that the energy within his healer's hands is a positive one, and that the negative energy of his doubts is unintentionally fighting off that positivity.

He relaxes.

"Good" encourages the nurse as her patient drifts away into a much-needed tranquillity...

A soothing voice gently tells Jack to wake up.

He opens his eyes to again find Aneisth's pleasant features shining down on him once more.

"How do you feel?" the healing nurse asks in a voice of tender care.

Taking a minute to regain his bearings, the newcomer sits up and tries to find the difference in how he is feeling now until the penny suddenly drops.

"I can move again! And sit up effortlessly! I've never felt so light!" he tests out some of his new movement by cautiously mobilising his feather-light limbs.

"Thank you so much, I feel great! What did you do?"

Whatever the elegant nurse had done seemed to have washed away all that was choking the life from him.

The flattered healer's demeanour becomes even warmer, if that were possible, and in her normal tone of gentle courtesy tells him.

"As you know, our science is holistic. So to put it simply, I used the science of nature to cure your infection. And not a moment too soon I might add."

Noticing her patient looking up to the ceiling's crystal, his mind still filled with questions, she realises that her explanation may not yet be finished.

"Would you like to know more?"

Her patient nods.

"Well the healing technique I used on you is called "irici", I'm assuming it's new to you?"

Jack nods again.

"Well, this method uses several approaches. First, I had to find a remedy

126

that would work for you, as it was you I was treating and not the poison.

"The galco crystal up there keeps the air free from impurities, while lending you its energy. Under it I massaged the poison from your lymphatic system, and used the correct oils and herbs to counter the rumery's toxins. I found that zingiber was your friend here, so it was the main driver in bringing you back to full health. The herb seems to have fully restored your fire.

"You will find yourself running to the toilet quite often over the next few days, but don't worry that's normal, just your body getting rid of the excess toxins and keeping you from heating up too much."

With her patient's curiosity satisfied the nurse decides to help him find with the questions that he should have been asking, and she knows just where to begin.

"Don't you think you deserve a rest every now and then?"

"What do you mean?"

"I mean the tension you hold on to would have finished you off if the rumery hadn't."

"Tension?" he responds, genuinely puzzled "Where did this tension come from? I'm living the dream."

"This tension's come from your own mind Jack. You have been competing far too hard with yourself, trying too desperately to bury scars that no longer exist."

Immediately Jack knows what Aniesth is referring to.

Although he is now living the life which he had always dreamt of, he also still holds onto the nightmares of his past.

'There was no survival of the fittest in my old time. Just a rigged game where evil would always win, and the best of us would starve for being a threat…

I was helled into that nightmare, and the people around me were so unpleasant. I'm glad I had my dreams of hope to carry me through…

But now everything is different, everyone gets to contribute, and no one is left behind. The leaders here look after everyone, they even create more leaders…'

A lightbulb ignites within his mind, and the newcomer finally accepts at an emotional level that the past truly is gone.

The scars which he believed to be irreparable, the ones that had always stayed at the front of his mind, were healed. He even pictured a blinding brightness fading the darkness of pessimism away into the peaceful bliss.

The storm had passed, within and without. The war was over.

He looks to Aneisth and without even having to connect with her, finds that he is now able to see the nurse's deep-cloudy aura, a peach colour that surrounds her physical being.

'It's amazing how much the world changes when you let go of hate.'

He looks to his gentle healer in sincere thanks.

"I've been hanging onto the past for far too long now, expecting all the good things to fall through like they always did before."

His expression becomes stronger, and far more resilient as he continues.

"But those days are past, and that's where they'll remain. No one is left behind now and the best get recognised, but most importantly; I feel I've finally found the place where I belong, a place with friends that I can call home."

Aneisth smiles at his near instant progress *'He has such a sweet willingness to change. What a boy!'*

"That's it Jack!" she applauds "I think you're going to do just fine."

Time Goes By
Part VIII

The atmosphere on this warm spring day is a still one of peace, there is not a breeze to be felt in the air, not a cloud to be found in the sky.

From a tree in Larutan's orchard, Jack picks the last apple needed to fill his basket for tonight's prep at the Hub.

He examines its crisp golden skin, admiring the shine before placing it atop the rest of the bunch.

"Hey there!" calls a bright voice from the hills overlooking the grove.

He looks over to see a very upbeat Gela coming his way.

Her purple aura beams radiantly and going by the unbreakable smile she wears, Gela has some good news to share.

"You look happy" he comments as she reaches him.

"I'm always happy" she replies playfully "Though I am all the better to see that you've made a full recovery from that rumery berry. What are you doing in the orchard?"

Jack admires his basket.

"Chef Yendo has me picking these for dinner. He says the ones we don't use tonight will be made into vinegar."

"Very nice…" Gela replies casually, doing her best to procrastinate from sharing whatever is on her mind, all the while looking ready to explode from containing her excitement.

'What is she trying to hide?'

Finally, the urge to share the news overwhelms her disciplined silence, and the nurse decides to come out and say what she has to say.

"Congratulations Jack!"

Perplexed, he raises an eyebrow, smiling at the apparently welcome news.

"Congratulations eh? Now where have I heard that one before?"

Playing along, the kind nurse cheerily shakes her head, all the while smiling at his cool façade.

"Last time I congratulated you on becoming a newcomer. This time, I'm congratulating you on no longer being one!"

"...?"

This raises even more questions for Jack.

"You're one of us now! Not that you weren't already. But now you've lost your training wheels and are ready to fly, figuratively speaking of course."

This sparks his curiosity further and baits him into asking the follow up question.

"Lost my training wheels?"

"Thought you'd never ask!" says the nurse with a wink, clearly hoping that he would continue with his many questions routine.

"Old Acki has left the Hub's nursery kitchen to travel the world. So now we're in need of someone to take his place... can you think of anyone better?"

131

"Me?" he asks in astonishment.

"Of course you! Your efforts haven't gone unnoticed you know. We all think that you're the person for the job."

A warm feeling tingles within his stomach, he does not know what to say.

"A penny for your thoughts?" asks Gela.

Jack's cool exterior breaks at this question.

He holds back his tears of sentimentality and hides them well, but the softening of his features, along with the change in his demeanour tells the nurse all she needs to know.

In a gentle voice, one breaking with emotion, he manages two important words.

"Thank you."

After thanking Gela and being assured the nurse would still be a part of his life, Jack receives an impassioned hug from his friend and mentor, then sets off to the Hub with his basket of apples and the good news.

He makes a few stops along the way, his first port of call being Thyn and Wey in the fields.

Both his friends are overjoyed when he tells them the news. They celebrate his good fortune with a roar of cheers and triumphant laughter. Jack also learns that Wey too is no longer a newcomer, apparently Gela had visited his friend before coming to see him.

Wey tells Jack that he had been put in charge of three sections of the fields, and that he and Thyn plan on starting up a streaming school in the near future.

"Sounds great, I might give it a try once you're up and running!" he tells them encouragingly but without committing, for Jack knows that he may be in for busier days now that life has moved forward.

Next Jack seeks out Yendo who he knew would be ki training before work.

He follows the energy which he could sense in the air and it soon brings him to the Crag en-route to the Hub, where upon the rocks, he finds his sensei standing in meditation.

Yendo uses calm gestures with his well-built arms to create clouds of light around his hands, which also causes the rocks around him to levitate. The cloud colours appear to be different from Yendo's aura, while generating a breeze around the sensei's hands in the still spring air.

With his basket of apples, Jack climbs the rocky ground to bring his teacher the news.

Despite being in the middle of something, Yendo notices his pupil's approach and welcomes him in his customary calm manner.

"Hi Jack, I'm practising cloudy arms here. Did you know that there are only a few people in the world who can do this, and most of them are sages?"

'*His abilities know no limits!*' he thinks admiringly.

The sensei allows the light surrounding his hands to dissipate before giving Jack his full attention.

"But you didn't come here to look at my sage clouds now did you? To what

133

do I owe the pleasure?"

Yendo asks this with a kind smile, as if he already knew what was coming.

"Thank you for allowing me interrupt your practice Sensei. I have some good news and I've come to share it with you straight away."

Yendo looks even happier at his student's excitement.

"I'm no longer a newcomer!" he says to his teacher "They're going to get me started in the Hub's nursery kitchen!"

"Congratulation's Jack, I'm honoured that you would tell me so quickly. Could you tell me who "they" are?"

"They...the community. I expect you might have something to do with it?"

"I might have, but ultimately it is you who has earned this for yourself. Your efforts would have been wasted in your old time, luckily you did not let that affect how you do things here and now."

"Thank you, Sensei."

Jack had never felt so complete. Consensus within his community, along with some hands-on tests of his abilities had gotten him the perfect job. This would allow him to reap the greatest rewards from a calling where he is best suited to make the most valuable difference.

A bright optimism engulfs what the former newcomer now sees when looking forward to this new chapter in life.

Melody

A noted improvement which Jack liked most of all in this new world, is that the people are mostly like himself, in the sense that they are all genuine. They even gave him something to aspire to by showing him their new level of kindness, simply in the way in which they live out their day to day lives.

'Who would have thought that love would become so fashionable?'

He would consider this while looking to those around him in the never-ending sun. However, unlike fashion, this kindness would not fade away into obscurity over the course of time.

The former newcomer settles comfortably into his new role in the society which he has now come to call home. Settling in was easy when the person he would meet one day was the same person who he would meet tomorrow, regardless of the situation.

He was given the opportunity to meet the children and nurses who he would be serving before starting out in the nursery.

At first the thought of meeting them made him nervous, particularly because he was unaccustomed to children, having never had any in his life before.

Jasper ran off at first sight of the young ones, Jack knew all too well how she felt, however once he got talking to them, he discovered that they got on brilliantly. He valued the little people's innocence and found that he was able to make them laugh and join in their games. He was even able to impart some of his knowledge on to them and enjoyed teaching them.

Being accepted by the children and their nurses made this new chapter in life even sweeter.

Jack always liked to be organised. One day after having prepared enough food to last the nursery a week, he uses the extra time created to spend with a boy in the nursery called Phaeder.

Phaeder, who had come to be Jack's faithful sidekick at his new job, thinks the world of the cool big kid who always had time for him. Jack also holds Phaeder in the same high regard, as the boy was everything he wished he had been when he was that age, so charismatic and good humoured. Hanging out with his young friend at work, whenever he was not in the kitchen, always served to brighten his day.

Jack's little friend laughs away at his good-bad jokes, causing one of the nurses to look over at them, giving him a warning look of *'You better not overexcite the boy',* meanwhile Phaeder rolls on the floor in stitches at another punchline.

"Hey kid, how many fingers am I holding up?" says Jack, extending all digits on his hands, flexing them to show that thumbs are to be counted too.

"Ten!" the boy replies.

"Wrong, I'm showing eleven."

"Eleven?!"

"Yes, look here…" he says, proceeding to count his fingers.

"Ten, nine, eight, seven, six, on one hand. Plus! One, two, three, four, five, on the other. Six plus five makes eleven. You can't argue with that!"

Phaeder again rolls over laughing.

'Numbers are strange, so easy to play with.'

Later that day Jack bumps into Gela in one of the Hub's many corridors.

Recently the two of them had become "passing ships" and only got to see each other during jams at the Space, which was hardly the best place to talk shop.

Both are happy to see each other having gone so long without the pleasure of the other's regular company, and immediately catch up on what's happening in their lives.

Jack tells Gela about how he is doing better than he expected to in the nursery. Everyone loves the food, which is great because love is what the food is made with. He also tells his former nurse of how surprised he is to be making such good friends with the children there as well.

"You always were a good role model Jack" compliments Gela, before going on to tell him that she is now working with three newcomers, none of whom are anywhere near the level that he and Wey were at when they first arrived.

Gela moves on to tell Jack, who is still flattered by this comment of an upcoming music festival which is to be held in Larutan in the coming weeks.

"It's gonna be a big one!" she says "There's going be lots of people from all over Larutan, and many more coming from further out. Word is, there's even going to be people travelling here from the furthest parts of the world, just for this."

Jack is stoked to hear about it, he had been becoming more and more confident with his gradually improving musical ability, and this would give him something new to practice for.

"Sounds like it's going to be epic!" he says, with the same enthusiasm he had for knowledge on his first day.

"What kind of music will be played?"

"That depends on how everyone is feeling when we come together. What kind of music are you hoping for?"

"Something energetic, I want to make some excellent riffs!"

"So you'll be taking the shred then?"

"No, the theleon"

"The theleon? You're gonna have a hard time making riffs with that" says Gela.

"Yeah, and I'm gonna love every minute of it!" answers Jack, with a devil-may-care grin.

Word of the festival had spread throughout the town in practically no time at all. All of Larutan was in a high-spirited frenzy in the lead up to the big event and it seemed as though everyone, without exception, was filled with excitement.

Jack had observed the people around him growing happier with each passing day, even his quieter counterpart Wey had begun taking music lessons from Gela at the Space, and like streaming, he was picking it up like a natural.

Jack even found himself giving music lessons to the three newcomers who his former nurse was guiding these days.

'And Gela said I was young for a newcomer!'

All three of the "next gen" newcomers; Yleot, Senwa, and Quaor, look years younger than Jack did when he first arrived, so much so that he found himself asking if he ever was that young.

'Perhaps "next gen" will catch on like "tortie"?'

The former newcomer had come on well as a musician. By no means a prodigy, or even an expert, but all the same he was happy to help, and more ironically, he was happy to answer all of their newcomer questions.

"So you're telling me that people don't vote anymore?" asks Yleot, the slim boy with quirky mannerisms, who tasked himself with getting to grips with the imbre.

"That's correct Yleot" answers Jack "Voting limited people's choice. It also disregarded the wishes of the losing side. Now we live in a world where if people's wishes were to differ, which they rarely do as selfishness is long gone, they will come to a consensus that all can agree on."

"Speaking of politics, where does the sewage go these days?" asks Senwa, the precocious girl, who had taken to the scalc, a keyboard version of the shred.

"Haha! I dig the association!" says Jack.

The three newcomers may not possess their old memories, but they certainly did have the instincts from their former lives.

"Our sewage goes into tanks that are filled with plant life that perish the waste."

"That sounds very simple, I was expecting the sewage to be transported by a big ship to some far-off place" says Quaor, the large boy with a rascal air about him who had keenly taken to the drum.

"No, but we do have trapes. They're like a modern-day cargo ship that can only be piloted by a sage. They're gigantic and hover above any surface; land, ice, water…"

Jack has a good time teaching the newcomers, and he finds it bizarre to believe that his questions were ever as persistent as the many they present him with.

The big day finally arrives and Jack is impressively alert for a person who had spent a near sleepless of anticipation.

He goes over to his bedroom window to get a good look at the people flocking en-masse, to what is currently being referred to as "Rainbow Beach".

Many from Larutan were making their way down to the sunny music festival, but he also notices people from neighbouring towns, and from further afield too.

With a rush of excitement, he quickly eats the food he prepared last night for a sharp exit today, gets himself dressed, being sure to swing his portable theleon over his shoulder, invites Jasper up onto the other shoulder, then hurries out to join the movement.

Everyone he comes by in the crowd making their way to the beach nods and smiles at him with such warmth and familiarity. A tranquil energy fills the summer scented air and all is quiet in the build-up of what's to come.

It reminds Jack of the expectant silence observed by those on roller-coasters in his old time, after the carriage had slowly reached the top and waited, ready to plummet down without warning.

The crowd reaches the happening and Jack can see that it's not only the beach where the festival goers are meeting up, but also the surrounding grasslands.

He soon makes his way through the throngs of music lovers in an assertive attempt to find his friends, which unfortunately summons his awkward side.

Although everyone here is friendly and having a good time, he still can't help but feel lonely and isolated within a multitude of people who he is unfamiliar with. He even feels peripheral without the company of the friends he is accustomed to, as if the kindness from the festival goers were merely superficial pleasantries, rather than a meaningful welcomes.

'No one told me the crowd would be this dense! I feel like I need to fight through to get somewhere quiet.'

Jack considers this for a moment then shakes his head.

'What am I thinking? These are good people and I'm in no danger! Now make like them and live in peace!'

No one had ever been this pleasant to him in his old life, now everyone was kind, so why is he complaining?

'Sour grapes.'

It appeared that memories of isolation from his previous life, although far from his attention, may still lurk somewhere down the shadowy recesses of his mind.

His demeanour becomes a lot more defensive, causing him to show even less expression on his face than usual, whilst using even swifter movements. His façade becomes more severe, yet he yearns so deeply to share a moment with true company here and now.

Though emotionally cold as ice on the outside, with everything short of having his arms permanently folded as he makes his way through the crowd, on the inside he dances a ballet of emotion through the warm aura which breathes within him, while longing for the friends who will end the loneliness.

Jack recalls the lesson that the Waterfall of Knowledge had given him.

He pauses for a decent count to reflect upon that lesson, knowing that a person can never fully reflect on their thoughts in a snap instant.

142

After a few moments of "reliving" the Fall's teachings, Jack decides to defuse his emotional turmoil, which only he was putting himself through, starting off with a breath as long as the fall's perpetual crash.

'I'm living happily ever after now. The people here are nice to me. There's no need to be scared. Everything's good.'

Continuing the search for his companions, now with a clearer mind-set, he comes across a stall which stands alone amidst the crowd on the grass. It is stocked to the brim with footwear and enjoys a steady intake of visitors coming and going, all looking happy from their time there.

He approaches the stall to find it run by a large man wearing the most stylish clothes he had ever seen in this life or the last.

'Fresh!'

Jack gets talking to the stall owner who is both very friendly, and a little on the timid side, despite being dressed for a dance-off.

"It's nice to meet you Jack. My name is Hanri the tailor" says the fashionable stall owner, showing a shy but welcoming smile.

"I'm set up here today, to give out these waterproof boots to whoever may need them. It's a dry day, but you never know how the ground will hold up under all this foot traffic."

"Wow! That's a new level of goodwill even for this place!" replies Jack.

"Ah, I see you're not long reincarnated" notices Hanri.

"Well I'm no longer a newcomer, but yeah, that's my story." admits Jack having been found out.

143

With undivided attention and friendly words, Hanri explains his "new level of kindness" to the former newcomer.

"As you know, our society exists for all to help one another. So, I'm happy to put my efforts to good use here, as I know that they will not be wasted. No one here will abuse my kindness, and I know for a fact that all the people here will help me if I need it."

"That's really good of you" responds an impressed Jack, not knowing what else to say before quickly moving on to more light-hearted banter.

"So you're a tailor. What'dya make of my clothes? Are they festival-worthy?"

Hanri studies Jack's clothes for a second then smiles.

"Those are some fine garments you have there, in fact, that t-shirt is one of mine. Though I'm not sure it's claw proof" jests the tailor, signalling "hello" to little Jasper with his warm expression. He extends a hand for the cat to get his scent, and after being accepted by the lofty sidekick on Jack's shoulder, invites the former newcomer to try on some footwear.

Jack is immediately fascinated by the shoes. They're like the sports shoes from his old time, the kind used for running, only these ones have ankle support too that reach up to touch the wearer's knee.

He tries on a few of the boots at the stall owner's kind invitation, and after trying on several shapes and styles, settles on a light-grey pair with lime-green piping.

With his chic new shoes, Jack asks Jasper what she thinks, and of course as a cat Jasper is not interested.

"If only we had shoes for you" he says to his furry companion, who doesn't appreciate the comment, but would not dare jump off to walk around, even when the crowd is as observant as they are here, her instincts told her not to tempt fate.

Hanri generously takes in Jack's sandals for him to pick up at the Hub when the concert was over, and after thanking the tailor for the boots, along with offering to bring along some nice food to his workshop tomorrow as a token of gratitude, Jack moves off.

He finds that some of the more audacious musicians had already begun playing within the crowd when he comes across a theleon player with cyber-yellow hair and emerald-green clothes.

The theleon player is not only able to create amazing sounds with his vase, but also uses his instrument to create unusual light shows in the air using the tones of his aura colour.

Jack had not known that so many colours were possible within a single aura. The musician skilfully uses the bright mists of his soul projecting from the theleon's vase, to create stories of a wandering dog in the air above him.

The musician appears to be well known among the festival goers going by his popularity and familiarity with them. Evidently Jack had managed to find a celebrity in this future, but what impresses him most about the theleon player, is not the fame, he seldomly ever let popular opinion sway his own. What impresses Jack is how charismatically the musician carries himself while performing. So cool. He even considers emulating the musician's hairstyle.

Watching the story of the dog as it walks through the scene created from the artist's energy, makes Jack consider how amazing the power of music is.

'I don't even know this guy's name and he doesn't know I exist, yet because of his creation I somehow feel like I know him.'

Jack continues his wander to find his friends, and while wandering comes by more performing musicians throughout the grass and on the sand, each showing off a unique skill much like "Mr Cool's" visual story of the dog.

Eventually in an area where tables and chairs have been set out for people to rest at, Jack spots Oclea sitting alone.

All tables are full except for Oclea's, where the enchanting twin proudly watches the world go by from her lofty throne of solitude.

He also spots a young man of his age, from another town, tentatively wandering through the tables at a snail's pace, timidly trying to find a seat.

Nearly every seat is taken and the young man's nerves seem get the better of him whenever a vacant seat would appear.

It relieves Jack somewhat to see that he is not the only one who is nervous today.

He watches the boy continue to wilt away after plucking up the courage to ask if he can join someone. That is until he comes by Oclea.

The boy stands awkwardly near the alluring twin's table, unsure of how to ask for a seat. He hovers about her table, ready to ask if he may join yet

146

pulling away each time he goes to ask. The twin notices him straight away and his hesitance eventually causes the carefree tortie's patience to erupt.

"Will you sit down already!" commands Oclea.

Doing as told, the nervous boy sits down across from the playful rogue.

"How you doin'? I'm Oclea" she says, raising a fist for a welcome bump.

"Hi, I'm Andis" the boy shyly replies, raising a balled fist to oblige.

A devilish smile quickly spreads across the mischievous twin's face, and Oclea gives his hanging fist a solid punch before he is ready.

Andis flinches at the impact and recoils to nurse his tender hand.

"Sorry" says Oclea, her spirited grin spread wide like the Cheshire-cat "I was asserting my authority."

Jack manages to stifle his smirk from witnessing what is comparable to a cruel, albeit, harmless cat, playing with a frightened mouse.

'Ah! Classic Oclea!' he thinks, going over to join them, hoping that his presence would put poor Andis at ease.

Oclea is pleased to see Jack, though a little peeved that her first acquaintance with Andis was being interrupted, while poor Andis who remains nervous, is reluctant to speak to Jack.

The tortie calmly greets the former newcomer, introducing him to the boy, then informs him of where he would be able to find Thyn and Wey on the beach. Apparently the two were spreading word about their upcoming streaming school.

Jack thanks Oclea and warns her to play nice with Andis, before leaving her with her new friend (or victim), as he sets off to catch up with his two streamer friends.

It is a fair walk down the busy shore, but sure enough he eventually comes by his high-flying buddies and the sight of them on Rainbow Beach is something remarkable, albeit very peculiar.

Like the many musicians Jack had seen playing before the main event today in the balmy sun, Thyn and Wey are exhibiting a strange performance, and though their show may not be as refined as those other performances, it certainly does push some boundaries in an effort to draw a crowd.

Wey wears a metal shred glove, but instead of making music in the space around him, he plays it into a theleon that sits before him. The music from the theleon's vase sends up a scattered lightshow into the air, in which Thyn highlights his lofty "gyroscope" for all to see.

Unfortunately, the visually bizarre act comes with an overwhelming droning noise from the shred-theleon mix.

They have a few spectators, but Jack reckons they would have much more if their "music" wasn't so intrusive to the serenity of Rainbow Beach.

"Hi guys!" he calls to them, after the last of their spectators had moved on.

"Jack!" shout both boys in boisterous welcome.

"Quite a show you have here" says Jack encouragingly, though with a slight hint of sarcasm due to the noise.

"Yeah man, we've had lots of interest!" says Thyn, as he comes back down to the ground.

148

"It looks like we're gonna' have a few new guys at our first class" adds Wey.

"Great! So you jamming using the shred-theleon combo tonight?" asks Jack, hoping he would not have to hear that noise again.

Wey looks to the instruments.

"Oh no! This is just a way of getting attention for our streaming gig. Tonight I'll be using the shred itself. How about you?"

Jack shows off the portable theleon which he satchelled to his shoulder.

"Nice!" comments Thyn "I'll look forward to dancing in your aura's green mist."

"Thanks" Jack says, then asks Thyn "So you're not playing anything?"

"No, I'm just here for the banter" replies Thyn, with a wink alongside his never faltering smile.

The boys wind up spending most of the day on the beach enjoying the music shared by all.

At one point, on their quieter part of the sand, little Jasper even becomes brave enough to run off and acquaint herself with some of the other four-legged festival goers, free from the worry of being accidently stepped on.

The boys are soon joined by Mantha and Miggles, who bring along some food from a stall further down the beach, then later, they are all joined by Oclea and Andis, who apparently got on very well together.

Despite no longer feeling isolated, now that he had his friends with him, and from enjoying the good times with all of the people on Rainbow Beach, Jack still feels a little out of place due to the event's disruption to his daily routine.

He looks round to see a small group of people hanging out nearby. Among them is a short woman with dark skin, wearing an elegantly loose rose-coloured robe, next to her is a pale man from Larutan, with short blonde hair and light plain clothes, and next to him is a tall man dressed entirely in black, with many piercings and a bright green Mohawk hairstyle. Seeing these individuals with such sharp contrasts in appearance, enjoying one another's company truly is what it's all about for Jack.

'*This is my town, a place for everyone, where everyone is accepted and differences are celebrated. Truly "come as you are"!*'

At these thoughts he finally makes peace with the disruption to his routine, leaving him with nothing more to complain about as the day had now become perfect within as well as without

So far, the music had only been played by a few individuals within the crowd, but as the evening drew closer, those individuals quietened down in preparation for the main event.

As the sun begins to set while the last of the late comers arrived, Jack catches sight of a peculiar bird walking along the beach.

He watches it for a moment illuminated in the twilight, pondering where he had seen this large bird before. The answer to its identity was on the tip of his tongue, he knew it was familiar in some way but struggled to recollect why. Privately, he works up a playful stress as he grapples with his memory, until it finally dawns on him.

"No way!" he gasps out loud.

"What is it?" his friends call over, wondering what was so shocking to the former newcomer.

"Over there" points Jack, keeping his voice low to avoid scaring off the bird.

Thyn looks over and realises what caught his friend's attention.

"You mean the dodo?"

"Yeah... dodo..."

"So this is the first time you've ever seen one?" asks Thyn.

"Yes, they're all supposed to be gone" whispers Jack, now quieter from disbelief than from consideration for the bird.

"Come now" mocks Thyn in a playful tone, as he comically waves a finger "Did you really think that the Earth only brought humans back?"

Jack did not know what to say. It made perfect sense that the Earth would reincarnate all beings and not just humans, now that he thought about it.

The group jovially laugh in good natured empathy for him, having had yet another of his pre-suppositions thrown out by something better.

'Man I love being wrong about these things!' he thinks, loving that everything now is better in ways that he never before imagined.

Soon after Jack's bird-watching episode, the group are joined by Emba from the Hub along with her friend Aegel, a girl of Jack's age with calming blue eyes, who at first sight wins his full attention.

Jack cannot believe it when he first catches sight of Emba's friend. She is the picture of the girl he would always fall for, the pretty and intelligent girl he believed he would never get to meet in real life. Butterflies scatter round the very core of his being, as he looks into her gorgeous eyes from the other side of the group, the story told by their sparkling blue lets him know that she is from a beautiful place, which is not so far away.

'Who are you? I'd really like to know. Would you like to know me? ... Listen to me talking to myself! I've never felt this way before!'

Emba finishes introducing her friend to the group, and the conversation is cut short when the sun abruptly disappears to submerge the festival in complete shadow.

The carnival atmosphere vanishes along with the last of the evening's glow, and all that can be heard now, is the concerned voices worrying over the light that has been lost.

A few minutes of vigilant murmurs pass in the darkness until suddenly, from out of nowhere, a blinding bright light fills up the entire sky. It dazzles every last person on the beach causing their murmurs grow louder.

'There's only one sun in the sky and this is not it, how can this be?'

As the glare begins to fade, leaving behind enough glow to see through the dark, the curious whispers dissolve into an excitable quiet. All stand in wonder of what will happen next.

The people in the crowd become sheepish, not knowing what to do, until a musician on the beach breaks the silence with an enthusiastic scream when they notice someone walking in over the water.

The festival becomes motionless as the crowd pause, looking out to see who this mysterious person walking toward them could be.

The moment creates a stillness so quiet that a pin drop would be easily heard by those on these shores of soft sand.

The stillness and anticipation lasts until finally someone shouts the name "Piliph" for all to hear. The name means nothing to Jack, but the festival explodes into a frenzied uproar at the sound of this name.

The former newcomer had never known that celebrations of this magnitude where possible, even the biggest celebration from a league winning sports goal in his old time had nothing on this.

Again, he is pleasantly surprised.

'The truth is beautiful…'

"Who is this?" he asks Mantha who stands next to him.

"That's Piliph. He's one of the most celebrated sages in all the world" she replies over the din.

Overhearing the conversation, Wey quickly cuts in with his own question.

"Are all sages this revered?"

"Oh no. Piliph is possibly the only person on Earth who can summon a welcome this grand."

"So what does he do to earn it?" asks Wey.

Thyn catches the question and chimes in.

"Oh, you'll see!"

Piliph walks over the almost perfectly still water, barely leaving so much a ripple beneath his steps as he travels across the sea, which is swayed only slightly by the tranquil breeze that wrinkles its calm surface.

As the sage reaches the beach, he raises his hands to gently cool the crowd's excitement, then gestures for them all to prepare for the music.

Those with instruments pick up their tools and stand poised, waiting with bated breath for their maestro's cue.

Piliph then raises a hand which is gloved with a unique looking shred which appears to be made from glass rather than metal, then pauses for a moment.

He keeps his gloved hand raised in the air as if charging it with energy, until he swings his hand down to create a riff that has the people on the beach screaming in adoration.

A shockwave of white light surges from his shred's wake, closely followed by a barrier of melodic sound.

As soon as the sage's creation hits the crowd on the beach, the people begin to join in.

An orchestra builds something wondrous, as those using instruments blend with all those using their voices to hum a sweet heavenly jazz of diverse sounds. Their music is blended to create a sound which truly brings Jack to the safe place where he belongs.

Along with the beautiful sound comes a light from the collective aura of every peaceful person playing music on the beach. It turns the darkness into a new day as they mix their radiating colours into the happiest tone the night sky has ever known.

Jack uses his theleon to create a placid tone, one which was far from the screaming riffs he had in mind when going in today. He wonders what could have made him instinctively play such a tranquil melody instead, surely there was more to this than trying to escape Wey's noise from earlier. It could not have been the inspiring sight of Piliph playing either, for although the sage's music was easy on the ears, his fingers looked like snakes rapidly darting about at near invisible speeds.

He then looks over to see Aegel, the girl he had only just met, and realises that she is the reason why he is playing so harmoniously tonight.

It is as if he already knows this person, her presence is a comfort to him. Already he admires everything about her, from her kind blue eyes and soft gentle features, to the welcoming bright yellow of her aura's radiance.

Jack is interested in Aegel, but not infatuated, and wise enough to know the difference as he continues to guide the green shapes of his aura into music.

As he looks to the girl to whom he is so magnetically drawn, his aura begins to judder in the midst of making music.

The green light from his soft melody plummets then spikes in erratic cycles, the colours fade away to burn brightly again, until finally it becomes a constant colour once more, glowing brighter than ever, only now with the cooling blue light of an ocean breeze.

Not knowing what else to do, Jack continues to play, while those around him look on in awe at his wonderful transformation.

The show goes on and the people continue to sculpt air into beautiful sound, only now with the urge to move overwhelming many, including Jack, who down their tools to come together in a great circle on the beach and dance.

Like the sounds from the musicians and the light from their harmonic auras, the dancers too blend as one. They hypnotically move in time, using the same motions to the music as one organic ring.

The dancers auras all blend together and create a burning ruby light which blazes above them, with the intensity of a bonfire which reaches as tall as the sky.

Jack breathes in at the sight of this glowing red cylinder that he found himself dancing in.

'People are so interesting now and we all share in something this special... I could only dream of this thing before!'

He begins to well up a little as he realises that he has finally witnessed his idea of humanity's perfect spirit being fulfilled.

He even catches a glimpse of Jasper outside the circle, singing along in a group with Uily and the little pig from the dojo, all sounding like little angels on the periphery of the crowd.

Luckily his tears of joy quickly pass without anyone noticing and allow him to focus on the moment instead of his internal narrative.

Looking to those making music around him and to those who dance away to the heartfelt rhythm of the circle, Jack understands that the music here,

156

which is far better than any music he has ever heard before, has connected everyone. At least in this moment, the people's hearts and minds have melded together, forming a brotherhood which celebrates their differences, and their shared passions, in joyous triumph.

Eventually as the festival's concord reaches its crescendo, Wey shoots off into the sky, streaming through the dance circle's fiery aura whilst holding out his shred glove.

His metal instrument rips the red dance-aura sky as he passes through, creating a billowy wake of multicolour above the festival goers, every spectator looks up in awe at witnessing his spectacular stream which marked the peak of this epic jam.

'They called it "Rainbow Beach" for the festival…'

"No way!" shouts Oclea.

"Yes Wey" retorts Jack, unable to pass on the liberty of such an opportunity for word play.

The music along with the rainbow cloud soon fade after a beautiful night which could have lasted forever, however, the people remain and with stronger spirits, long after the music had vanished.

With the musical aura gone, the sky was now a shade of turquoise so dark it was almost pitch black. But in this dark sky were large white clouds with gentle notes of tangerine, gradually passing through.

To Jack, watching the clouds pass in blissful silence was like watching his own thoughts pass by unobtrusively in the distance.

Not much could be heard now as the festival goers bask in the ambiance left behind by the night's melody. Jack and his friends remain calmly camped out on the beach smiling.

When looking round to his friends who lay on the sand around him, he finds that he has a lot to say yet feels no need to say any of it.

'Life is good'

He then looks over to find Aegel, looking back at him with fondness in her tranquil blue eyes.

'Life is better' he says to himself, loving that his feelings for someone could be so strong that they would change the very colour of his aura.

He wonders if either he or Aegel would pick up the courage to talk to the other tonight.

Their group is eventually joined by Gela and Pat, who had taken part in the orchestra from further down the beach.

Jack is impressed by Pat's wheelchair tonight, a machine clearly built for comfort, with sturdy back support and wheels fit for the sand.

Gela tells the group that her ukulele was her instrument tonight, while Pat had jammed using his imbre.

The group eagerly share their experiences of the night, and Gela is very relieved when she learns that Jack had chosen to join in tonight's tranquil melody, rather than play the energetic riffs he had mentioned when they last spoke.

Being told of Jack's transformation, along with Wey's rainbow, impress both

Gela and Pat.

"I don't believe it! Rare doesn't even begin to describe an aura change!" his former nurse declares with spirited enthusiasm at the news.

Very soon the conversation moves over to streaming when Wey asks if either of them had managed to catch sight of his rainbow.

"I saw it Wey" says Gela with a smile "I'm no fan of streaming, but your rainbow cloud was really something up there."

Pat tells Wey that the rainbow will have gotten some interest for the upcoming steaming school as well. He then then adds.

"I wish I could be up there with you on opening night… but I'll be up there again. Someday."

At this a confident voice, in an even tone, calls over in a volume that is subtle, yet audible to all.

"I couldn't help but overhear you there. Perhaps I can be of service."

The group look over to find Piliph, the sage, walking towards them.

He moves so elegantly over the sand, with such perfect poise whilst leaving no footprints behind him. Jack notices the sage wears unusually squared baggy trousers, which hide his leg movement as he "glides", making him question if Piliph was walking or if he was actually gliding through the air.

No one knows what to say as the sage stops on front of the wheelchair to kneel and speak with Pat at eye level.

"Pat isn't it?"

"How do you know my name?" the man from Larutan asks, his eyes widening with the wonder of the many possibilities of how the sage could have known.

"Like I said – I couldn't help but overhear."

After deflating the otherworldly expectations of Pat and the rest of the group, Piliph goes quiet for a moment, not smiling, but projecting good feeling all the same.

He stands up and looks to Pat, nodding to the man in the wheelchair in kind friendship. Any anxieties which Pat may have carried are disarmed by the sage's friendliness.

"You say you would like to join your friends here when they take to the skies?"

"Yes" Pat nods "I'm very close to a full recovery, but I need more time."

"No more."

Piliph reaches out and places both hands behind Pat's neck whilst taking in a deep breath. A light emanates from the sage to surround both himself and Pat.

The light is much like the light that Piliph had sent out at the beginning of the concert, a light too colourful to be white, but too white to be multicoloured.

It appears to join the two men, but not in a connection as Jack understands them. Everyone present stares awestricken and unsure of what this could be.

The two remain as silhouettes, encapsulated by the brilliant pearl light for a short while, until the light soon fades and the group look on in silence.

'What just happened?'

Suddenly, a commotion stirs as they all bear witness to something spectacular; Pat rises from his chair to stand up on his own two feet.

A silent pause prevails, as everyone realises what has just happened, before they roar in a communal cheer.

Good times of congratulations and celebrations are shared by all, and amidst the hubbub, Jack is approached by the sage.

"I saw your transformation during the concert tonight, it was very impressive."

These words flatter Jack, who despite never seeking approval from anyone in this life or the last, finds praise from such a revered individual to be quite the honour.

"Thank you" he answers, not sure of what else to say.

"Watching you change like that put me in mind of something I'm working on."

"What is it?" asks Jack, eager to learn more about the sage's work, however Piliph's attention soon wanders when he notices Emba standing just behind the boy with the new blue aura.

Emba had just finished talking to Thyn and inadvertently joins Jack's conversation, when she turns round to see whose eyes she could feel on the back of her neck.

Both Emba and Jack wait for the sage to say something, then after an

161

awkward minute the quiet is broken with a peculiar question from the sage.

"Neither of you realise yet, do you? You don't realise who you both are?"

The two look to each other in perplexity as the sage benignly smiles.

"Here..." Piliph raises both hands and gifts Jack and Emba with a shared connection using his crystal white light.

The world outside of the light disappears, leaving the two to exist in a realm of their own essence.

Despite being different from the tangible world in which they live, this realm is a very comfortable setting, one that feels like home to both.

Jack catches glimpses of Emba's life through her lively pink aura. It is a proud and happy journey, one completely free from trouble, which leads to now, the moment where she looks into Jack's life through his new blue aura, to see the forest, the Hub, the Waterfall, and the beach.

The serene connection between them is comparable to the most blissful meditation on an empty beach, like listening to the sweetest song while living a dream filled only with love.

Jack remembers how close he had become with Wey after knowing him from their first ever connection. From that moment on he and Wey had become the best of friends, but this connection here with Emba is different. The feeling is so much more, but why?

In a flash, the two of them visit Jack's past where he questioned the very nature of existence, instead of simply *"playing the game"*.

It is an isolated life and a cold one filled with hurt, right up until the end on

162

that day in the hospital.

After witnessing how he lived, Emba moves in closer to Jack, placing a hand on his shoulder.

"You poor thing" she says with beautiful compassion.

Though revisiting his past is far from what Jack would have wished for, it does not torture him like it had when the Fall took him there.

This time he watches the past with his eyes instead of participating with his mind, which enables him to see it from a new perspective, a perspective which allows him to see more than what his own two eyes had seen when living back then.

That world still represented all which he is not, but now "living the dream" as he often liked to say, and looking back on it from this point in time, Jack is able to see that a lot of good had existed back then. And though those torturous times had been harrowing for him personally, he can now see a certain beauty to his story back then.

'I once heard someone say that "all the world is a stage, and the people are actors" …I played my part commendably.'

He watches and watches, learning of the things which had eluded him while living back then. Realising that although things are far better now, his past had been made worse by all the negativity he shrouded himself in because of the evils he was subjected to.

'I thought that utopia was on our doorstep when I was growing up. The world was going to be a great place when I became an adult… I was crushed

163

when I learned that those expectations had been a far cry from the truth. A disagreement over something trivial with my parents got so out of hand that our relationship became toxic. I could no longer remember the good time we shared, even came to believe those times had been false. But I remember now. You were my family, we had lots of good times, and I love you - your Mijo.'

A tear filled with nostalgia runs down Jack's cheek, before he and Emba are transported again, this time to another place within their strange connection.

The time it takes them to now is in Jack's former home after his death. His parents are older now, wiser too. They have decided to embrace life and have learned from their mistakes. They now have a little girl, she is healthy, she is beautiful, and sharp, she is also good natured and alert. Looking at this intelligent beautiful cherub fills Jack's heart with joy and gives him precious hope for the world he once lived in, then suddenly he comes to a realisation. She is Emba!

In another flash both Jack and Emba are brought back into the present, where they once again stand on the beach, surrounded by friends enjoying the good times.

The two now look into each other's eyes not knowing what to say.

'Emba, the reincarnation of the little sister I never knew...'

Tears fill their hearts while the friends around them disappear to a world outside this moment.

"Brother?"

"Sister!"

They come together to closely embrace the most cherished thing that either has ever found, neither let go, as if making up for all that time lost from spending lifetimes apart.

'This changes everything. You're my sister. I love you, and I'll do anything for you.'

"Jack..." Emba sobs, finding a peace within her being that she had never known possible in her wonderful life.

With her dormant past-life memories unlocked and having come to terms with this new side of her identity, Emba is now able to tell Jack what happened in his old life after he departed.

"Mum and Dad were so broken up over losing you, it hurt them so bad. They raised me as best they could, as if they were atoning for the mistakes they made. They loved me, and they never stopped loving you."

This was so much for Jack to take in that he didn't know how to react. He didn't have the best relationship with his parents, but he did vividly remember being loved in the end. He is also glad to hear that his old time had treated Emba far better than it had ever treated him. Apparently she experienced the positive parts which eluded him when he was around.

These past revelations take their toll on Jack who becomes emotionally exhausted from it all. He sits down wishing that he still had the energy to continue conversing with his sister, but "Thank you" is all he manages, unable to articulate beyond those two important words.

"I'm glad I could help" she replies, fully grasping the world of love behind her brother's laconic gratitude.

After a brief recess, the two compose themselves and begin to engage with the rest of the group again. Such good friends. They all knew that Jack and Emba were going through something, so they respectfully gave them the space and time they needed.

Jack see's Pat stun his audience by healing a small cut on Wey's arm just by holding his hand over it. Evidently the ability to heal like this was new to those who have always lived in this era.

Pat looks to his hands in wonder.

"Did I forget to tell you?" calls Piliph, "When I healed you, I also passed on the power to heal. Now our young friend Wey here also has that ability, but I must warn you both that this will soon pass."

"Pass?" asks Pat.

"It is much like a muscle; it needs nourished and exercised regularly to work, and there are not enough injuries to maintain that."

The entire group look to Pat and Wey, astounded by their gift from the sage, if "gift" is the correct word.

"Well Aniesth certainly has an easier job for a while!" announces Pat, bringing about a roar of good-natured laughter.

166

While everyone shares the merriment, Jack and his sister take the moment's distraction to approach Piliph.

"You really aren't scared of upsetting the order of things, are you?" Jack says to him.

He asks this with a positive smile, referring mainly to the revelations concerning himself and his sister than to the miracle of Pat's health.

The sage simply smiles at the boy who had grown so much over the course of this one night, then asks.

"What has it told you about your world Jack?"

This is the perfect question to ask him this evening, so perfect in fact, that it catches the young man off guard.

"What a thing to ask me!" he replies, attempting to buy some time to articulate his thoughts after such an exciting journey.

He quickly scrambles his thoughts for the words which would credit where his life is tonight.

Searching his feelings, he channels the energy within his hands, thinking with his whole body and not just with his head to find a timely answer.

"It's revealed to me that this world has never been perfect, but it has always been ideal.

"The world I lived in was sickening, but my negativity was always mine. That old society might have shown me the door to dark places, but it was me who walked through them. I'm so happy to have left that all behind. I've learned a love for a sister who I never knew existed. All living things are family to

167

me, but Emba... she is something special, and the love I have for her proves that!"

His sister looks warmly to him, her heart filling with joy at his words of reconciliation, words which would have not been possible had it not been for her presence here tonight.

The sage again simply smiles knowingly, yet humbly, then in a blink of an eye vanishes before them.

Jack and Emba both look about for the missing Piliph, wondering where the sage could have gone, but nowhere can they find him. All they manage to see are their fellow festival goers and the first of the new season's snowdrops beginning to fall through the sky.

A Change in the Wind

Goodnight summer
I barely knew you
As you die
Part of me dies with you
I'll always remember you
Will you remember me too?

"So he just disappeared like that?" asks the enthusiastic child.

"True story Phaeder. He just vanished in the split second I blinked. Apparently, sages can do that."

"Wow! That's so… Wow! Wish I could have seen it Jack!"

"I'm sure you will one day. You never know, you might even be the teleporting sage."

"What's teleport?"

"Well… it's getting to where you're going without having to travel."

"That would be good too, but I like travelling, it's part of the fun."

Phaeder's words bring a smile filled with pride to Jack's face.

"You're wise before your time my friend."

Once finished at the nursery for the day, Jack meets up with Gela and Miggles to go watch Thyn and Wey's first streaming class.

They approach the snow covered clearing where it will all take place and find the turnout to be very low so far. Jack could only see two new hopeful flyers.

They also find the familiar faces of Liss and Aneisth in the small crowd who had come to support their streaming friends.

Even though only two new people had come along to participate, an undeniable anticipation still prevails in the air today. Wonder from the streamers, along with wonder from their spectators, fills the moment. However, this wonder does nothing to alleviate the anxieties of Jack's party, particularly those concerning Pat, who had become invincible since being healed despite having yet to stream with his new-found health.

With upbeat laughter and bravado shared amongst the experienced flyers, Thyn briefs the new guys.

Miggles quietly leans in toward Gela who stands behind Jack and asks her.

"What are your thoughts?"

"It should be fine, but I still worry. I'm just glad the sage gave them those healing powers."

"Yeah, and I'm glad Aneisth is here too" replies Miggles, looking over to make sure the Hub's healer nurse is still there.

Both new kids nod in acknowledgment to Thyn's final instructions before he claps to bring quiet to all present.

"Thank you all for coming! This is a big day for us and happy that so many of you have come to see us off!"

Some applause comes from the audience.

"Today we have two new flyers, Tipiter and Atio, and the return of Larutan's very own skyman; Pat!"

An encouraging applause comes from the audience for the two new boys, followed by an even grander applause for Pat on his long-awaited return to the sky.

Thyn continues.

"These are perfect numbers for today, as it will let the more experienced streamers partner up with the guys who aren't used to this, and for the moment that does include you Pat."

Pat gives the young speaker an accepting thumbs up along with a carefree grin.

"Now what you've all been waiting for, we're gonna take to the sky!"

Some cheers come from the spectators as Thyn pairs Wey with Tipiter, Oclea with Atio, and himself with Pat.

In pairs they levitate off the ground, drawing more applause as they go up two by two.

Before long all six are in the air, earning ovations from their audience as they fly above the spectators in circular formations.

"They did say they were going to put on a show before shooting off" comments Jack to no one in particular, words that appear to fall upon deaf ears.

"Pat is going too fast for his first day back!" Gela says, almost to herself, as she watches the streamers break away from the show circle to fly freely in their designated pairs.

Jack takes note of the nurse's words and agrees. He pays close attention and notices Pat's fast and loose movements, especially when he and Thyn vie to overtake one another.

The six streamers eventually return to the frosty ground to thank everyone for coming along, which is the spectator's cue to leave, as the flyers would now be travelling far from sight.

Wey and Thyn go out to thank their friends personally for coming along, and when receiving their heartfelt thanks up close, Jack finds that his two friends are positively glowing from the success of their first class and not just from the chill of the cold sky. He is happy for them and at the same time, a little disappointed in himself for not being up there too.

Once they part company, he hears Thyn warning Pat to take it easy. It was reassuring to know that the instructor had also noticed what he and Gela had seen from the ground this afternoon.

While making his way to the Hall tonight, Jack stops to look out through one of the Hub's many windows, out onto the cold panorama where a tranquil scene of snow-covered fields fills the view.

172

The virgin snow which lay deep over the land, brings with it a silent beauty as its makers dance serenely through the evening air. Tonight families throughout Larutan unite within their warm homes and peace fills the streets as though no one else existed in the world.

Jack finds the snow, which made the darkness brighter, to be very calming.

'It's like a sunlight in winter, here to help you find your way'

He comes back from his thoughts with a smile before going on to "prestigiously dine as a guest" as he often liked jest now that he no longer worked in the Hub's kitchen.

His friends, old and new, are already there when he arrives. All are pleased to see him, especially on this cold night where the good times are shared by everyone. Jack is also sure to send on his compliments to Yendo and to the chef's new helper, Quaor, who had expertly helped his sensei with tonight's preparations.

The night goes by smoothly. Jack enjoyed the spicy potato stew and had many laughs in good company were he and Miggles played off one another's jokes and one-liners all evening. The two kept those around them entertained and even had Gela laughing so much that she was to the point of tears. That is until suddenly, just as Miggles was finishing off a punchline, an awful sensation swept the room piercing Jack's soul.

Without warning he becomes cold to the point of shivering. Something was wrong in the world and he knew it without thoughts. His fingers freeze up like ice, while a dead weight pulls him down into a void where no one would be able to lift him from.

"I feel it too!" says Miggles.

Apparently the two boys are not alone, for the entire hall had shifted from a warm harmony relishing in good times, to a commotion over the spreading sensation.

Gela catches the attention of both the boys. Tears filling her eyes, not the tears of laughter she was fighting only moments ago, these tears are very different.

With a lost expression, she quietly tells the boys.

"I think I know what's happened."

Gela had hoped to be wrong, but her instincts had proven woefully correct.

Jack and Miggles follow her out to the Crag on what had felt like the longest journey, through the cold, where they find Oclea and her streaming partner Atio.

Both just sit there at the bottom of the rocks crying uncontrollably, staring into space with shock drawing their gaze to a faraway place.

Gela asks the two what's wrong, but Oclea and Atio are too lost within their nightmare to answer, and understandably so, going by what could be felt in the air.

She notices the two weeping streamers are avoiding the higher level of the Crag, to the point that they kept their backs to it. Clearly what caused so much distress would be found up there.

174

The nurse sends Jack and Miggles on ahead while she tends to the broken flyers.

Jack hurries up the rocks at a pace which leaves his breath trailing behind in his footprints.

'You should have taken it easy on your first day back!' he snaps, preparing for what he will find when they reach the top.

When he and Miggles finally get there, out of breath, after what had felt like a disproportionately steep run, they find someone kneeling down on the snow-covered plateau crying.

The two continue to hope for the best whilst instinctively knowing better.

The person kneeling hears their approach and turns to see them.

Jack and Miggles draw closer and once the boys are recognised by this lone figure, he speaks in a fragmented and hollow voice.

"Migs… Jack… … There was nothing I could do…"

It was Pat, only this was not the Pat that Jack had come to know.

Instead of the energy filled gent with a mischievous sense of adventure, always ready for smart witty talk, this Pat was broken and forlorn. So much so that Jack almost did not recognise him kneeling there on the snow.

Both boys look to where Pat is crying, and it takes a moment to register just what they are seeing exactly. Maybe it was denial trying to spare them the trauma, but they soon come to realise just what it is they were witnessing.

"No! It can't be!" Jack cries out in a hoarse whisper.

Miggles reacts with a silent despair.

175

Laying before the forlorn Pat's knees is Thyn, just resting there, lifeless.

"What happened?" asks Miggles.

Pat gathers himself, he puts his thoughts in better order, then with a long-bereaved sigh tells them.

"We were pulling some fancy moves up there… I came down for a rest and Thyn stayed up. His skills were something else up there… A strong wind came from nowhere and threw him into the rocks… I tried to help him, but these healing powers were useless… He died in my arms!"

After speaking, Pat again breaks down into an uncontrollable grief.

Giving him a moment, Jack decides to move closer to his fallen friend.

Thyn looked so peaceful lying there, not moving.

It isn't right to Jack. Thyn is always trouble free, never a worry on his mind, always full of life, always moving, playing, helping. Thyn is always running off to his next adventure with his winning smile. This couldn't be Thyn.

Like Pat, Jack drops to his knees beside his friend who lay motionless.

'You were such a great guy, the most alive person I ever met. You had so much to give… I wish it could have been me and not you.'

He futilely tries to resuscitate his friend, pressing the centre of the breathless chest, hoping…

Pat and Miggles say nothing as they watch Jack try to save their friend.

Eventually Jack gives up, having done all he could, it just wasn't good enough to bring Thyn back.

He calms a little after the initial shock and brushes his fingers down the side of his friend's face. This would likely be the last time he would ever get to touch Thyn. His skin was as cold as ice.

'I considered you a good friend, but we never as close as we should have been and it's my fault. I was always too cool and severe for my own good, always worried about getting hurt. I should have known you better, like Wey knows you. Please forgive me Thyn.'

Jack tries to distract himself from his sorrow and looks out onto the view of the forest without leaves, cold and hollow. The slightest drop of rain touches Jack's head and he welcomes a downpour, not out of bitterness, but in the hope of washing this terrible episode away.

Thyn's body was taken back to the Hub where it would remain until his funeral.

The following day was sunny, a sharp contrast from winter's smog-white skies of everlasting cloud which dulled the atmosphere since the festival.

These were difficult times for all, especially Oclea, who upon noticing the weather, made the understandable outburst of how wrong it was for the sun to suddenly be there now that Thyn was gone.

Oclea's sister puts a comforting arm around her twin, who would normally have been full of mischief on any other day.

The episode had been so shocking for Jack that he was no longer sure of anything, which was very unlike the boy who never did anything without reason.

177

He tried getting by through making himself a pillar of support for his friends during their grief, it was the rational thing to do. But he felt his efforts were useless as all his friends were lost within their own distress and not ready to return.

All the same, he does try to comfort Oclea with his well thought out words.

"It might be fitting that the sun's out today. Thyn loved the sky, and now the stars have a new angel shining down on us."

She does not reply, Jack only hopes that his words helped a little.

It was a good thing that the people of Larutan generally worked such short weeks when compared to the workers of his old society. As well as improving everyone's wellbeing during normal times, it also made covering the roles which were usually carried out by those grieving much easier, while they took the time they needed.

Oclea, Thyn's friend and fellow sky buddy had become increasingly irate since losing him. Snapping at anyone who would speak to her, which made Jack begin to suspect that she may have liked Thyn as more than just a friend. A pointless academic thought.

Jack's counterpart, Wey, who was perhaps Thyn's closest friend, did not say much. He had always been such an emotional individual on the inside, yet like Jack, rarely showed his feelings on the outside, which helped him maintain a calm façade, but now he appeared distant and quieter than ever.

Mantha, the mother-hen of the group, handled her grief superficially well whilst busying herself helping others. However, Jack had growing concerns that she was overworking herself into her own early grave with all she was doing. Her care for the group made him wonder how Thyn's parents, who he had never met, were coping with this.

Miggles, was no longer the chatterbox everyone had come to know and love. Though teary eyed, he would provide a shoulder for his friends to cry on while not saying a word.

It was there for all to see that Pat was beside himself. He talked away from time to time, even tried to banter like he used to, but those who knew him well could see the change, that something was now missing from his life.

Jack noticed that Yendo the Sensei was there for anyone who wanted to talk, but he also noticed that Yendo the man did not say a word.

Nurse Gela kept going, albeit outside of her role at the Hub, keeping the rest of the group strong while taking a break from her usual duties. Most people would have never known that she was grieving, however those who knew her best, especially Jack and Wey, could see the difference under her professional exterior. Especially when they looked into her jade-green eyes, where they could see her pain and loss behind the caring smile she still wore.

The funeral came quickly enough, which was a godsend as the days which had went by between it and the incident, had felt like a bleak eternity to

Jack. Far worse than when he relived his distant past inside the Waterfall's abyss.

Jack had only felt cold since finding Thyn. Cold and nothing but cold. He continuously shivered from his icy bones, all the time whilst trying to find a reason for any of it. A reason to make this tragedy meaningful, a reason to explain why it had ruined his perfect life. If there was one, he certainly couldn't see it.

Though he does realise now that as unkind as his past life had been, he had never had to deal with death before, other than his own of course.

'Goes to show that the bad things will always catch up with you, even if its thousands of years later.'

People had come from all over Larutan, and further afield, to pay their respects. Jack is impressed with the huge turnout, and until now had no idea that Thyn had made an impact on the lives of so many.

The service itself takes place on an open plain which is thankfully free of snow on this unusually dry winter's day.

To celebrate his life and passions, Thyn's friends from Greenleaves, headed up by the visitor boy, come streaming in above the procession which carries his body out to the service. The mourners below find it wonderfully fitting that their lost friend should receive such a unique send off from the people who knew him best.

Thyn's body lay peacefully swaddled in cloth on a bonfire that had yet to be lit, surrounded by a large circle of chairs many rows deep.

'So Thyn is to be cremated?'

Jack discretely leans over to Mantha to ask if cremation was the norm for funerals now.

"There's no norm for funerals" the twin answers in a solemn tone, before she kindly explains that each person has a service that is unique to who they were, often at their own request.

"So Thyn requested this?" he asks, wondering if his friend had given the subject much thought while he was alive.

"Not in so many words" sobs Mantha "but the people who knew him best, know that he would have wanted this. His vapours will travel through the sky and his ashes will be cared for by the elements."

The arrangements for Thyn's funeral made sense. It even comforted Jack somewhat to know that his friend's service should be such a fitting reflection of the great person he was.

The proceedings begin when a sage named Enti, who was conducting the ceremony, calls for everyone to be seated.

All present take their seats, and the turnout is so great that all seats are filled with many more people having to stand behind the giant ring of chairs.

The sage mainly talks to the crowd about coping during times like these, though his words are lost on Jack, whose thoughts are of how his day to day life would never be the same again.

The sage's speech is a short one, which pleases Jack as he did not like the idea of someone who had not known Thyn speaking at his funeral. It gets him thinking that the people here did not belong either, they were not there with Thyn at the Crag like he was. Though he does accept that to begrudge them for not being there on the night was petty and unrealistic, even he might not have been there had it not been for Gela sensing what happened.

Next Gela addresses everyone. The nurse tells them of the time she had first met Thyn in the Hub's dining hall, and how she knew from that moment on that he was going to be a great person from his winning smile and willingness to help.

After Gela, Thyn's parents address the crowd, and then his best friend Wey.

More people give lovely anecdotes of the fond memories they have of him. Beautiful stories, and the more Jack learns from them, the higher his estimation of his departed friend grows.

His thoughts wander off to the first time he had met Thyn.

Thyn had welcomed him so openly with his winning smile, and after he and Wey had learned how to connect, Wey had found that Thyn was a sentimental ladies man who was waiting to find his one true love. Jack had taken it for granted that Thyn would someday bring home "the one".

Yendo steps forward with a burning torch after the speeches finish and lights the bonfire.

As the flames grow up through the pyre, the grieving crowd in the seats rise to their feet to create a heartfelt thunder of applause in honour their friend. Jack could feel the love and gratitude from everyone in the ovation which celebrated Thyn's triumphant life, the sincere and thankful recognition of how he had enriched all their lives with the simple gift of knowing him.

The dust settles and the days go by after the service, and though those grieving had managed to find their way back into their normal routines, life now was still not normal enough for Jack.

He carried on helping at the nursery and in the fields, from time to time stopping to wonder what Aegel might be doing. He would occasionally go to the dojo, and sometimes the Space, but he never saw his friends as often as he used to.

Sometimes he would see Wey when he was out in the fields. Wey was still the friendly athlete, though somewhat different in character now that he had lost his best friend and given up flying. He was now more polite and reserved.

Jack saw Mantha from time to time at the dojo where they would harness their ki under Yendo's tuition.

With the help of ki, Mantha had become brave and resolute enough to make it through those trying times, and now that it had all been put to rest, she had come out stronger than ever.

However, Jack never saw Mantha's sister anymore. Apparently the mischievous Oclea had resumed her job looking after the children but had fallen away from her social circles.

He no longer saw Miggles either. Jack had heard that his once talkative friend, who had gone quiet during their period of grief, was now spending more time at home with his family.

Gela was still around. Jack would often see her in passing at the Hub or at the Space on the very rare occasions he went there, but they did not talk much anymore. That is until today.

As Jack was heading home from the Space he hears the nurse's tender voice calling after him.

He stops to let her catch up and notices that her jade-green eyes are bright once more. She had clearly healed from the darker days.

He could now see her spiced lavender aura radiating voluminously through the air around her, the purple glow now as strong as it always had been.

Gela smiles calmly to her former newcomer-in-training, then asks him one simple question, a question which is normally a mere pleasantry with a prescribed response. But when asked it now, Jack can feel the conviction in her words.

"How are you?"

Despite feeling the nurse's warmth, and the affection of the question's sincerity, Jack honestly could not answer, not even to himself.

With a little encouragement, he eventually manages to talk about his feelings, but they confuse him. Despite having a well-rounded life, he still cannot help but feel a sadness since the loss of Thyn, a sadness which brings with it, a cold and empty loneliness.

"You said there's still challenges in this society. I didn't fully appreciate that

184

'til now."

"I understand what you're saying, it has not been easy."

'Don't I know it!'

"This is the first time you've had to deal with losing someone isn't it?"

Jack nods.

"It was so unexpected. I'm no expert on bereavement, but if your friends and routine here in Larutan aren't bringing you back from the sadness, then maybe what you need is a holiday."

'A holiday?'

Jack had never contemplated going on holiday in this new paradise he had awoken in. Why would he need to? Now, he found the answer to this question which he had never asked.

"Where would I go?" he enquires with a growing interest in getting away for a while.

"Well that depends on what you're looking for."

"How about someplace warm, with people?" asks Jack, knowing better than to go somewhere isolated while feeling blue.

"Off the top of my head, there's Yellowround, a town not too far from here. Though it might not be as warm this time of year."

Jack considers this and everything else that has transpired lately.

He was fortunate to have such good people close to him, supporting him through the trying times. No one should ever have to deal with grief by themselves. But now that the proverbial storm was over, he figures what he could do with now is some time away.

He brings his full attention back to Gela upon deciding that a break might do him some good, agreeing that a trip to Yellowround sounds like a plan.

His answer makes the nurse smile, she is glad to hear that he would take the respite he needs.

"Great! I'm happy to hear that. Though Yellowround is a fair bit away if you're travelling alone. Would you like me to see if someone will go with you?"

Jack considers the question for a second then decides that he will make the journey himself.

When Gela asks him why, he simply smiles for no apparent reason then answers.

"It's all part of the fun."

The Journey

The frosty road could have gone on forever from what little could be seen through today's mist.

The shadowy trees to either side of the road, stand naked as forsaken memorials to the life that once flourished around them. They tower ghoulishly erect with branches twisting out to create a sight which evokes a feeling of cold isolation in Jack, akin to that which he had carried thousands of years ago, in the impersonal city of uncaring strangers.

He said his *goodbye-for-now's* to those who would be missing him and set off on this solo expedition.

It was sad for him to leave his friends and family behind, but he assured everyone, especially himself, that he would not be leaving for good. Unlike his old world, living in Larutan was through choice and not by circumstance. Life was good now and built on cooperation, and at last he had found people who he could love and trust. "People who he could love and trust" he hopes that it is not out of line for him to include Aegel in this, even though they had not yet talked with each other.

Jasper was very unimpressed to say the least when he asked her to wait for him. The little cat with those big gorgeous eyes pleaded with him to stay, imploring him not to go in the most heartfelt of their unspoken connections. An appeal which went far beyond what spoken words ever could and would always remain with him in memory. This made leaving all the more difficult for Jack, who had begun to question whether he was really making the best choice when becoming the recipient of her silent cry.

In the end his mind was made up, and with his flair for the dramatic prevailing, he stuck to his chosen course and set off on his own to fix his one problem, though only after assuring the outraged Jasper that he would be back. It was only a holiday after all.

So far Jack feels that the journey had already given him a little more room to breathe.

'I guess that's why I need this holiday.'

Despite the season, the journey to Yellowround had been a reasonably comfortable one. Jack had packed ample provisions and had come across plenty of fruits and nuts which had evolved to survive in the harshest conditions along the way.

'If only the tree leaves could do the same' he would think whenever he looked up. There was also freshwater in abundance to keep him going, if his bottle ran out.

On this journey Jack carries a tune which had been sung by the festival goers at Rainbow Beach.

It is a simple song of a journey not unlike his own now. He sings it and whistles while travelling through the rocky, snow covered paths, reminding himself of those better days when he had not a single worry in the world.

Even though there is no one around to hear, he still couldn't help but feel a little embarrassed for singing out loud in the open. It must have been the trees looming claustrophobically over him, looking bare and hollow as they stood out from the mist.

He moves forward with the keen curiosity of a young man starting afresh, but the wretched trees that stand void of leaves serve to remind him that all good things must come to an end.

It feels like forever since he last saw green, that precious colour of life.

The journey may have felt like a long one to Jack, but it also feels like a positive one in spite of the haggard winter trees. The spacious quiet gives him the perfect platform to introspect healthily, and he does have plenty of nice places to visit in his mind along the way.

Cartoons from his early childhood played through his head while on the road, distracting him from any negative thoughts that crept up on him. It gets him thinking about the nature of negative thoughts and the so-called entertainment from his old time.

The electronic picture boxes they used back then only ever seemed to bring about bad tidings. All negative dramas and horrors coupled with violence. It was no wonder his old society had been in the mess it was, even the books were centred around despair. Conflict will naturally grab any living being's attention, making them watch for longer out of an in-built survival instinct of observing a potential threat. To exploit this was crass.

Jack now realises that the input he had received back in his old life had affected him far more than he had ever appreciated. From this realisation, and the many others he had come to along the way on this first day of the journey, he feels like he already knows himself better.

'And if a person knows themselves better, surely they can better understand the world.'

His first day of travel proves to be a productive one.

Jack had managed to cover a great distance, and when it comes time to rest, he pulls a button looking object from his pocket, squeezes it in his fist, then simply tosses it out before himself as if feeding the birds.

The button explodes (actually quickly unfolds) into a comfortable tent made from very light, water-tight material, with fresh ventilation and better heat than a heavy-tog coat.

'The wonders of technology when it's used properly' he thinks as he rests up.

Tomorrow would be his second and final day of discovery on the road to Yellowround.

With fresh air, open space, and no responsibilities, Jack enjoys a blissfully deep sleep. The kind that will recharge a person completely. That is until he receives a strange visit.

As he sleeps, Jack's dreams take him to a large white room, at least it appears to be white.

In it he sits on one of the many loud coloured couches and waits. For what he is waiting for he is unsure, but he continues to wait all the same.

Someone enters and sits down on a couch nearby.

Jack looks over to this visitor and finds Thyn giving him an encouraging smile.

The smile carries a warmth with it, but to see his lost friend out of the blue comes as a shock, so much so that it stirs Jack's awareness, getting his conscious mind moving alongside this unconscious vision.

'Where has my dream taken me?'

The Thyn in his dream speaks straight after this aware question.

His voice as welcoming as it always had been, respectfully asks.

"Hi Jack. How are things now?"

Jack does not know what to say, his hallucination had just spoken to him.

Running purely on raw instinct he begins to laugh uncontrollably. This was to be the response to a dream visit from his dead friend.

'What's my mind doing to me now!' he ponders as his conscious and subconscious collide.

Dream-Thyn wears an expression of disappointment upon hearing the laughter, then suddenly, in the blink of an eye, Jack wakes up.

'What a dream!'

Immediately a shadow of guilt drapes over his shoulder. It had clearly been his own mind playing games on him, but what if it wasn't? What if sweet Thyn really had come through from the other side to visit him in a dream? He looked hurt by the laughter.

The sun rises and Jack readies himself for another day of travel.

191

Today the mist lifts to reveal an even deeper forest of desolate trees. The emptiness turns the pit of Jack's stomach into a basin of dread.

To give himself a change of scenery from the trees, he instead looks up to the frosty overcast clouds in bitter judgment.

'Winter. The brightest thing about it is the dull colours. I'd take that orange sky I want rid of over this any day.'

At one point on today's journey he manages to catch sight of a red squirrel scurrying about in the distance ahead. The poor thing looked like it was shivering from the bitter cold.

Seeing the bushy-tailed critter, which had become extinct in his old life, jogs some old memories from his childhood.

He recalls gathering bags and bags of chestnuts from the local park in competition with the other boys. This memory brings with it a pang of guilt, as he wonders if he had helped bring about their extinction.

"I selfishly took sack-fulls of your chestnuts home as trophies. For no reason, except maybe to keep up with the other boys. Did I deprive you of your food?"

He asks this as the beautiful autumn-red squirrel moves off, hopefully to find itself a warmer place in this forbidding season.

In the hope of helping it out, Jack lays down some of his seeds and nuts where he last saw the squirrel, then carries on his journey through the forest and his feelings.

He whistles a variety of songs from both his old and new lives, even re-

192

watches some more old cartoons in his mind while continuing his journey at a good pace.

'Can you believe it? A world that's safe for a young man to travel alone in! Life's way better without sick ones or those agents of dystopia doing everything they can to ruin a good thing.'

Before long he notices a figure coming his way from further down the road.

This fellow traveller in the distance gives him a wave, and against his mood, Jack returns the gesture, readying himself for some fresh conversation.

'Life is much easier when every stranger is a friend you have yet to meet.'

As they draw closer and he sees that this fellow traveller is a man who is perhaps a little older than Pat and travelling light.

"Hi there…" the man welcomes, his voice a soothing lilt which carries with it the wisdom of age.

The traveller's name is Coram, a very to the point man who describes himself as a "retired sage who had chosen to drift".

Going by what he tells Jack, in very direct sentences, this life choice has given the former sage many friends and adventures along the way.

Normally an individual's brevity would shadow their welcoming personality, however Jack finds the drifter-sage to be a great guy, and his frankness to be just a little quirk to his character.

Originally from the town of Netherdam, Coram tells Jack of how he had led a very rewarding life until the day he discovered that he had nothing left to strive for. When the sage realised this, he took to the road and enjoyed new scenery along with very few dull moments ever since.

Coram regales him with many stories of former escapades which are very entertaining, until the conversation eventually flows to Jack and his experiences, starting with his aura.

"That's an interesting aura colour you have there my friend, teal-blue, quite unusual."

"Thank you. My colour was originally mint green, then it became light blue, and now it's this."

"I see. You must have gone through a whole lot for your colour to change like that…"

Jack goes on to tell Coram about the events that led to his transformations, stories which were old news to him, but very fresh for the traveller who has a few questions over his new acquaintance's current choices.

"So you have a good life, and there's a girl you like, but you've chosen to be out here alone?" The former sage asks this with a blatant air of satire.

"Well, you're here and you left a good thing in Netherdam" responds Jack defensively.

"I lived my "good thing" to its fullest, now I'm out for more. But you… You haven't even started yet."

Jack knew exactly what the former sage was saying. Most of Coram's close friends were now gone, while most of Jack's friends where back in Larutan. With a sigh the former sage asks.

194

"Would you really choose to have problems out of some fear of being bored?"

"I do have problems" responds Jack, as he begins to take a more serious tone.

"Thyn is gone and everyone else has changed! They're still kind, but in my old time, kindness was a jewel to be cherished! Now everyone is kind, all the time, even now without Thyn…"

He stops there, a little embarrassed from the outburst, then recomposes himself with a relaxing breath.

The former sage gives the young man a moment to think about what he has just said. A very big moment which lasts until the sage responds.

"Remember you are not everyone else."

Such a simple thing to say, but the statement rings-true to Jack, who in this moment realises that he had lost a good friend just as the rest of his friends in Larutan had. They had all suffered just as he did, so why did he change? There was no need to change his life so drastically in the drama of dark times. Surely the commonality of kindness was a blessing.

Coram gives him an encouraging smile and he gestures to a nearby tree.

"Last winter this tree was a husk like it is now. But soon after, spring came, and it once again grew from being bare and decrepit to thick and strong. It will again be lush and bright with life. Our winters aren't the end of us my friend, they're just a small circle that you find when you look inside."

The tree nearby stands there quietly as it meets Jack's gaze.

195

Realising that he is the tree, Jack thinks back to the good times he had at the Crag with his friends, jamming at the Space, laughing as he worked away in the nursery's kitchen or out in the fields. Those days seem much brighter than today, which makes him realise that the dark rings in life's history only serve to make the light ones brighter.

Coram notices Jack beginning to come around.

"Your friend will be back one day, of that I am sure. Just look at you. It might not be today, or tomorrow, or even next year, but one day Gaia will return him to us."

The Earth does look after all things, and the idea that Thyn would eventually return is a welcome comfort to Jack.

"How will he exist until then?" he asks.

"You tell me boy, you're the one who's been there" replies wandering sage.

Jack of course, has no response to this.

'The wonders of mystery.'

Just then, giant flurries of snow begin sweeping in from nowhere, to absorb the dark view of the forest into a haze of smirry white.

"More snow! But winter's been already!" shouts Jack over the wild gale, clearly infuriated by the sudden rush of more artic weather.

Noticing the young man's distaste for the extended winter, and knowing the boy better than the boy realises, Coram decides to use his sage's cloudy arms for Jack's benefit.

"For you" says the sage wisely.

196

Coram begins to create puffy grey clouds from his hands, all the while steadily moving them round in interchanging loops.

The movements of Coram's arms are calm and tranquil, a soothing display which would pacify anyone watching, that is until he stops abruptly, to shoot a bolt of lightning skyward from the clouds in his hands.

The sky above them turns black, darker than the charcoal cloak which it had worn during the silence of the festival before Piliph appeared.

Here the sky becomes jet black enough to encompass even the whitest of snow which had so brightly illuminated all that it touched.

Jack looks to Coram, wondering why the sage would do such a thing, only to see a friendly smile looking back from the older man's face.

Rain begins to pour from the darkened sky at an alarming rate.

The torrents soak Jack's clothes and wash away the settled snow almost instantly, until finally, after months of never-ending whiteness, the ground could be seen again.

'Is this the end of the world?' Jack asks himself.

He takes cover from the storm under a tree with thick branches, whilst the deluge roars down with thunderous tenacity. He looks over to find Coram still standing in the same spot, still wearing the same smile in the rain.

From nowhere the sun emerges, and almost immediately it evaporates the wetness, making the landscape look as though the rainstorm had never happened.

The trees even start to bloom a little as the sunlight vanquishes the clouds.

197

Disregarding the bizarre situation, Jack steps out from under the cover and out into the sweet sunlit energy where buds are now again starting to bloom.

'*This is what it's all about!*' he thinks to himself, admiring the new pink and green flecks growing on the trees.

With his eyes closed he takes in a breath of the clean air and decides that it tastes better than it has in a long time.

He opens his eyes and delights in the new glow of the tangerine sky, though he did of course wish it were blue again, then it dawns on him, what he should do with his life.

Jack turns back to thank Coram, only to find that the drifter-sage had vanished. He smiles in reminiscence of how Piliph had made a similar exit.

'*Apparently sages can do that.*'

He continues to smile, feeling at peace with the new purpose he had discovered, then from nowhere a familiar voice calls his name.

"Jack? ... Jack? ..."

It sounds like it is coming from within his head, however he is not joined in any connection. '*What now?*'

Not wanting to be rude, he responds "Yes?" feeling a little foolish for talking to a voice that may well be imagined.

"Oh Jack you are there!" replies the voice, sounding so familiar, though he could not quite place it.

"It's me, Emba"

"Emba? You sound different in my head. Where are you?"

"I'm at home. You didn't know we could talk like this did you?"

"I didn't. Are you psychic?" he asks, curious about this new possibility.

"Haha no." his sister chuckles.

"If you have shared a connection as strong as the one we have, then you will be able to talk with each other over great distances. Anyway, I'm here to ask how the journey to Yellowround is going?"

'What a time to ask!' he thinks.

What are the odds that Emba would contact him now, the minute he discovers his new calling in life.

"Well actually I'm thinking of turning back, the travel itself seems to have done me some good."

"Oh we'll see you soon then! By the way I have someone who would like to talk to you."

After a very quick pause, a new voice enters the conversation.

"...Jack?"

'I know this voice, don't I?'

"Jack, this is Aegel, Emba's friend from the festival"

'Her voice is as beautiful as her complexion'

"Hi Aegel" he replies.

"Hi Jack, Emba's connecting us just now. I never got a chance to speak to you that night."

Loveliness flows in her words as she continues.

"It was such a good night and I've not been able to stop thinking about you since. I've never felt this way about anyone before, and I think you might feel the same way about me... Please tell me Jack, is this the real thing?"

His heart leaps. He can feel Aegel's sincerity and it is so wonderful to hear because he does carry those very same feelings for her. Jack would never use the word "love" lightly, however in this place in time, it feels as though the cosmos have aligned to bring the two of them together, even when they are a great distance apart. As if they had become vessels for two celestial entities who were always destined to be joined. All he wants to do in this one perfect moment is declare his undying love for Aegel. He wants to shout it loud from the highest rooftops, for all the world to hear, but of course Jack, the pokerfaced master of understatement, answers his affectionate caller with one simple, yet beautiful word.

"Yes."

Upon answering Aegel's beautiful question with his equally beautiful answer, Jack's teal blue aura begins to burn brightly again, just as it had on the night of the festival.

The blue aura now glows as bright as the sun above but does not stop there. The light which shines so brightly from his aura becomes a brilliance which makes his blue appear white with brightness.

Eventually his aura cools down to show a new colour, the true colour that Jack's aura was always meant to be, and unlike the weather in the sky above, this change was permanent, he could feel it.

Jack feels complete as he stands within the sapphire glow of his completed aura. It gives him the certainty that life will go on in Larutan and the blue sky would return.

The excitement gets to him and in this moment, throws aside his reservations and declares for both his sister and Aegel to hear.

"I have had the same feelings! I haven't been able to get you out of my mind either, even in the darker days. I want to know you Aegel... Would you like to know me?"

Happiness can be felt from everyone in the connection.

"I would like that very much. When will you be back?"

Exhaling deeply, his sky-blue aura flaring up to burn blindingly again, Jack is overcome by the impulse to run, and takes off in the direction of home.

He runs at a free and brisk pace, accelerating to unimaginable speeds that even a cheetah would not be able to keep up with, as the inferno of his aura's blue flames reflect off each other to envelop the borders of his sight.

Running at such extraordinary velocity, with his mind charging on ahead and a tailwind of ki sweeping him forward, Jack feels a new level of liberation, free from all the negativity which may have held him back before.

To his amazement, he gains more and more speed, whilst his sky-blue aura engulfs more and more of his vision.

Finally, all he witnesses with his eyes, is the calmness and strength of his own energy surrounding him.

There is a change in the atmosphere and in a snap instant, Jack halts his momentum, skidding across the ground to slow to a stop.

The stream of blue light which followed his trail, clears to reveal both Emba and Aegel standing before him outside the Hub.

The girls look to Jack, and two hearts become as one when his eyes meet with Aegel's.

Holding back their tears of joy, the two come together to embrace as if it were going to be the last thing either of them would ever get to do.

Emba gives the lovebirds their moment before finding her words.

"You teleported?" she gasps, her aura revealing the happiness she feels for the love they have found.

Struggling to find the correct words, Jack, with a smile, simply replies.

"Apparently sages can do that", while his aura decrees a heartfelt "Thank you" to his sister for making this moment possible.

Jack is unsure or whether he had taken his first step toward becoming a sage, or if he had help from a benevolent friend. Either way he spends no time pondering this, as there is more to consider in the here and now.

'All good things must come to an end, it's an inescapable fact of life, but so too is the fact that all the bad things must end too. It really is a beautiful world.'

Just then, the bright tangerine sky above them begins to grow clouds of darkest orange, as if readying itself for another vengeful storm.

The three look on to the ominous uproar brewing overhead, so intense that it shakes the Earth beneath their feet.

Together they huddle, unsure of what to expect, then as the three form an embrace to protect and comfort one another, a calm circle begins to open over Larutan.

The circle found at the eye of the crimson storm, opens wider and wider to unveil a soothing blue atmosphere behind the vastness of sinister red.

Jack and Aegel hold hands at the sight of this hope.

The colour and love of this cerulean dream continues to spread, until it spreads throughout the world. Over the highest mountains and deepest jungles, the calm circle travels the world over, until finally the Earth prevails, and the heavens in their entirety return to their long-lost blue.

The family of three standing outside the Hub tear up as they bear witness to the return of such magnificence, a beauty which everyone believed to be gone forever.

'Congratulations Jack' the former newcomer hears a familiar voice say.

'Piliph?' he asks, knowing this to be a telepathic communication similar to the one he and his sister had shared.

"Correct. Do you recall a project I mentioned to you at the festival?"

Off the top of his head Jack is unsure. He has a lot on his mind, understandably, and the festival was a good while ago, especially when time was twinned with emotion. Still, he traverses the corridors of his mind with some serious deliberation, but for something as notable as words from a sage to evade his memory was unheard of, and successfully it remains so.

"Yes I do remember! It took me a while, but I remember now. You said something about my aura when you mentioned it."

"I thought you might. Well thanks to you, that particular project is now complete. That sweet notion of your perfect blue sky made it all possible. Thank you, Jack, and please continue to be yourself. You are the only you, and that's exactly who we need in this world."

A humbled Jack takes in the sage's words whilst looking to the gorgeous sky. It is now blue, not that chemical grey which people had called "blue" back in his old time when the sun was out, but sky blue. This was the real deal.

Though Jack is silent, the tears of blissful closure he wears, along with the contented feeling of serenity which they carry, are felt by Piliph, wherever he was communicating from.

"One more thing before I leave you in peace" says the sage.

The words perk the former newcomer's attention.

In their connection Jack hears what Piliph has to say through the sage's feeling and not his words. The feeling from the sage tells him to look out beyond the horizon.

Jack follows the instruction and looks over the open plain, bearing witness to a vision in the atmosphere where the billowy clouds would normally rest.

Within the faint apparition in the distance, Jack witnesses his former self on the very same hospital bed where he had gone to sleep for the last time. Only the self he sees now on that fateful day wakes up, this time with a new lease on life.

His parents in the former time are so happy. They too go on to live a much fuller life, and together they all live as happily as can be, along with his cherished little sister who arrives not long after his miraculous recovery.

Only he appears to be able to see this incarnation, but Jack is sure that it is real, so much so that he knows it to be true. Yet he still exists here in this perfect future.

'How can I exist now, if my life back then has changed?'

Before long he wisely gives up on trying to explain something as crazy and contradictory as this.

'Mysterious ways' he says to himself, dropping the question.

"Happiness will be with you for a long time" he hears Piliph say in one last remark before the voice fades from the connection.

A simple sentence, but one which would stay with Jack for the rest of his life.

From nowhere little Jasper jumps onto his shoulder, bringing him back into the here and now.

"Where did you come from my friend?" he asks the faithful cat while lovingly stroking her head. He then notices sweet Aegel looking at him with affection in her starry eyes and love in her precious heart.

Knowing him so well from love alone, Aegel, with a smile tells him.

"Utopia begins with "U" and that's why I'm so proud of you! You feel this good because you've let go of your past and finally found peace."

As true as the blue sky above them, he had finally let go of the bitterness from his past, and with a content smile Jack agrees.

"Yes. My little Eden now has the perfect sky."

His words may have been about the sky, but the feelings they carry were for Aegel.

He thinks back to the negative musings from his visit to the Waterfall.

'When re-living the past I had said "What is the point in anything when everything means nothing" … No'

Within the peaceful quiet which the Earth has never before known, this blissful silence which only the wonderful rebirth of a blue sky could bring, a new smile dawns upon Jack's face.

'There is a point to everything because anything can mean something.'

Feeling humble and privileged, like he has finally arrived, with little Jasper on his shoulder, his sister standing next to him, and Aegel's hand in his, Jack looks over the fields of Larutan from the Hub.

With love in his heart, he summarises his experiences with Gaia in one last narrative.

'I'm so grateful to have lived in this world, even in my old time when I took it all far too seriously. The people were awful to me back then. But I realise now that I attracted it. And if one, one hundred, or even one thousand people cross you, you can't let it make you give up on humanity.

'Socially, it's all like a choir. We all must sing from the same sheet and work together to play our part. It's the only way! Life's all about learning; making mistakes and living to tell the tale. Thank you so much for having me Gaia. Thank you. And thank you everyone who has blessed my beautiful life by

coming into it. Thank you all without exception. The Heavens are in perfect balance, and we are still here on Earth…'

I am sensitive and imperfect

I wonder how the finished picture will look

I hear music from the soul

I see the beautiful now, the best time to live

I want this moment to last forever

I am sensitive and imperfect...

I pretend that I have always been as fulfilled as I am now

I feel the beautiful energy of all life on Earth course through streams in the

air

I touch the light within me and reach out to find it in others

I worry that the perfect now may one day come to an end

I cry when I look out to the beauty of hope that shines brightly in the world in

live in

I am sensitive and imperfect...

I understand that in the end love will always be there

I say anything is possible because everyone can change

I dream of what's still to come

I try my best for those around me, despite my flaws

I hope that peace will last forever

I am sensitive and imperfect...

...I am Jack

To Sharon,

Here is my story. It may suck but writing this got me through some difficult times (might have published an older draft here, as I've had to make many corrections since printing this).
Anyway. This story is an escape - it is intended as a state of mind to take the reader away from any troubles they may have, rather than being something to follow to find out what happens next.
Hope you find it okay, happy reading.

Yours without wax

Michael

Printed in Poland
by Amazon Fulfillment
Poland Sp. z o.o., Wrocław

68R00125